SHORT STORIES OF
JESUS

WILLIAM HAGER STEPHENS

WESTBOW
PRESS®
A DIVISION OF THOMAS NELSON
& ZONDERVAN

WestBow Press books may be ordered through booksellers or by contacting:

WestBow Press
A Division of Thomas Nelson & Zondervan
1663 Liberty Drive
Bloomington, IN 47403
www.westbowpress.com
844-714-3454

ISBN: 979-8-3850-1030-1 (sc)
ISBN: 979-8-3850-1031-8 (e)

Library of Congress Control Number: 2023919735

Print information available on the last page.

WestBow Press rev. date: 11/13/2023

Contents

Preface

My story is based on Scripture as found in the book of Luke. (All the Scripture quoted is from the New King James Version Copyright 1982 by Thomas Nelson Inc. Used by permission.) The remainder of the narrative is from the thoughts of the writer, which is fiction, or the imagination of the writer to make the story more real.

I am not in competition with Jesus the Son of God the best storyteller of all time. I am trying to tell you what was in the hearts and minds of the people who were with Jesus. The circumstances of being a follower of Jesus were different from what we are experiencing today. When they were baptized in the name of Jesus, they were saying that they were giving up Judaism and believed that Jesus was the Son of God. They were barred from the temple and the synagogue, children were not allowed to go to school in the synagogue, and they were ostracized from all society and lost their jobs.

Thanks to a merciful God whom I serve and who never gave up on me. Some of you know that I started this book two years ago. This book took a lot of research, which I really enjoyed. Then I was involved in an automobile accident that totaled my car and almost totaled me. I thank our Sunday School class or small group, which is led by John and Jo Smith, for the many prayers that brought me before God. (The small group is known as the Friendly Class of Northcliff Church in Spring Hill, FL.) God did not let me get hauled off as a total wreck like my car was. The accident left me walking with a cane and a head that had brain fog.

Thanks to my wife, Judy, for caring for me when I was helpless, and she still does. I'm grateful for the ones who encouraged me to finish this book: my friends in Winona, MN, David and Brenda Terpstra, my friends at our church, Jerry Bauman, his wife, Char, and her sister, Vickie Trinkle. Then we have people who sit on my pew almost every Sunday, George and Vicki Welling. My good friend of twenty years, Charles Suber, read the manuscript and said it should be printed. Charles' wife, Ruth Ann Suber, helped me with my first book, "How to Get to Heaven and Back," and helped once again with editing.

Chapter 1

THEOPHILUS

THE TASK

Luke 1:1–4

I was kind of bored today. Nothing exciting was happening. Everything around Judea was as it had been for the past few months. I plan to do some exercise take a hot bath, and then later meet with some of the officers for lunch, we would probably talk about Roman politics, and how good we had it before we were assigned here.

These Jews were different from the Romans. We, Romans, had killed them time after time and yet they would not be submissive to us. They only tolerated us. Take Jacob for instance who had prepared my bath. He had worked for me for two years, yet he would not eat with me. He would not work on the Sabbath day and he didn't want me to touch him. He was so religious that he had some kind of law to dictate his every move. I felt sorry for him. He was so courteous and followed my instructions as long as it was no law against it.

The Israelites were divided on what they believed. One group would go to Herod's temple to worship. People in the other cities would meet in synagogues. Then there was a group who believed Jesus of Nazareth was the Messiah they were looking for. They would meet in the Jewish temple in synagogues and sometimes in homes.

Their religion was so different that I sent my friend and physician Luke to Antioch to investigate carefully and write another story about the life of Jesus.

Lately, these folks have been called Christian: they were also taking in Gentiles. Luke will let me know soon. He was sure excited when he left, for he loved to write. He had all kinds of things written down. I sometimes wondered why he took up medicine. He sure was interested in the new religion. He believed that Jesus was Israel's Messiah. I thought so too but wanted him to write all he could about the things Jesus did. When he heard about Saul and Barnabas preaching in Antioch, he just had to go to hear them, and he promised to send me a written copy of the life of Jesus

I too was interested in Jesus for he had changed the lives of people who believed in him. They were not like the religious Jews here in Jerusalem but were loving and kind to one another and to all people. They were anxious to tell the story and to help those in need.

It was almost time for lunch when Jacob brought my mail. I was surprised to find a letter from Luke. He had been gone for several months. I just couldn't wait to read what he had been up to.

AD 60 most excellent Theophilus you are indeed a friend of God and a friend to me. Several biographies of Christ have already been written using as their source the material circulating among us from the early disciples and other eyewitnesses. However, it occurred to me that it would be well to recheck all these accounts from the first to the last and after thorough investigation pass this summary on to you, to reassure you of the truth of all you were taught. Luke 1: 1–4 (NLT).

When I arrived in Antioch I went directly to the synagogue and asked some people who seemed to be in charge where I could find food and lodging. Well, to make a long story short when they learned you were a friend to Saul several homes were open to me. I chose to stay at the home of Manaen who had been a playmate of Herod the Tetrarch when they were just children. The reason was that he had a large home with a large desk and many books. He even has a copy of the story of Jesus written by John Mark. As you might have guessed the journey here was the most exciting time of my life. Walking from Jerusalem to Galilee was good exercise. Why Galilee? Because that is where most of Jesus' ministry was done.

Even the city of Jericho had some stories to tell and I was hardly out of sight of Jerusalem. Walking through Pereau and Decapolis was a great source of help but Galilee really captured me. I met with his mother and brothers and sisters. In fact, I stayed a couple of weeks there and received information that had never been recorded before.

His mother is a marvelous woman. You should meet her when she comes to Jerusalem. Then I went on to Antioch and found a lot of wonderful people. They all seem to know the story of Jesus. I will write it all for you and send you a section at a time. By the way, I met a person named Paul, you mentioned that you knew him. He used to be a Pharisee and hated Christians. Oh! That is what they call believers in Jesus here in Antioch. He has a friend named Barnabas who is a wonderful person. More later. Luke

I laid his letter aside and I would read it again after lunch. Imagine Luke and Paul as friends. They must be the most brilliant people I know. Paul had a marvelous story on his conversion and I can just see Luke soaking in every word he said. I really must have my housekeeper Jacob read this for me. He loves to read Greek. Maybe it will soften him a little on what he believes. I have to hurry now, don't want to be late for lunch.

Chapter 2

ZACHARIAS

THE HAPPY PRIEST

Luke 1:5–25

Elizabeth and I have been trying to live a blameless life before God. We tried our best to always do what was right. However hard we tried sin still crept in. All we could do was follow the Law of Moses and bring the proper sacrifice.

Being a priest made it difficult to do. To admit I was a sinner and lawbreaker before God was easy. He knew me like no other. However, the people did not know me as God did. Dear God please forgive and help me.

This made me aware of my name Zacharias meaning God remembers. I also know He forgets when I sacrifice. Elizabeth's name means his oath. We love to put our names together; God remembers his oath and tries to figure out what oath he remembers. We like to think of Psalm 89 where he said David's seed would endure forever and his throne as the sun before him. It shall be established forever as the moon. We were looking for that one who would have an eternal reign.

It was time for me to go to Jerusalem for a week to take part in the sacred task of the service in the temple. When the lots were cast and I was chosen to burn incense on the altar I was really happy. This was the highest duty a priest could do and we could only do it once in a lifetime.

When the temple gates were opened and I was given incense that was smoldering, I prayed. Please dear God help me do the worship service as you have instructed us. And, dear God give me and Elizabeth a son.

Suddenly on the right side of the altar of incense there appeared unto me an angel of God named Gabriel. He told me not to fear. My heart felt as if it would jump out of my body. He told me my prayer was heard and Elizabeth would bear a son. He even told me to name him John. Now I had prayed this prayer many times and could hardly believe it was being answered. You see Elizabeth and I were both getting too old to have children. I asked him how was I to know this was true. He told me I would be mute until these things came about. Then he disappeared as suddenly as he had appeared.

Meanwhile, the people waited outside and when I went out to speak to them, I found I could not talk. All I could do was try to tell them with arms and hand signals that I had talked to an angel.

I had to stay in the city the whole week to continue my duties. I wrote my story and let the other priests read it. They were overjoyed that Elizabeth and I were going to have a son. He would introduce the Messiah to Israel. I had a promise that he would bring me joy and delight. He will also be great in the sight of the Lord. He would even be filled with the Holy Spirit from birth. When I returned home and stood before Elizabeth with the most marvelous news in the world, I found I could not speak. She knew something good had happened. She would soon know we would have a son and our son would announce the Messiah. I just knew she would cry when I told her, and she didn't disappoint me.

The angel had told me that our son would be great in the sight of the Lord. He would drink no strong drink. He would be filled with the Holy Spirit even from his mother's womb. He said that John would turn many children of Israel to the Lord. He would also go in the power and spirit of Elijah and turn the hearts of the fathers to the children. He would make ready the people for the Lord. Elizabeth and I felt we were the happiest people in the world.

Chapter 3

MARY,

THE FAVORED ONE

Luke 1:26–56

It had been a restful night but a little too short. I knew I would feel better after moving around, but I sat a while on the side of my bed because no one else in our house was up yet. The four baskets of clothes I had washed and folded for the soldiers caught my eye and I remembered why I felt the way I did. Perhaps I would bring home more when I deliver these. My hands felt as if they needed the rest, but tomorrow was a Sabbath and I was sure we needed the money more than my hands needed the rest.

It was while I was looking at my hands and planning the day's work schedule that suddenly a voice said, "Hail favored one. The Lord is with you! Don't be afraid Mary, for you, have found favor with God. Behold you will conceive in your womb and bear a son and you shall name him Jesus. He will be great and be called the son of the highest, and the Lord God will give him the throne of his father David and he will reign over the house of Jacob forever, and his kingdom will have no end."

I was scared because he was Gabriel an angel sent from God. I was also puzzled because I was a virgin and asked him how could this be. He said the Holy Spirit would come to me and the power of God would overshadow me and for that reason, the holy baby shall be called the son of God. Then he told me Elizabeth was going to have a baby in 3 months. He said that nothing was impossible with God. I believed him, after all, Sarah had had a baby when she was 90 so why should I not believe the angel of God? Who could I talk to about this? My mother would say I was dreaming, Joseph! What would he say? I had to go see Elizabeth that was the proof I needed. So, I told my mother and just as I expected she said I was dreaming. Then I told her that Elizabeth was going to have a baby in about three months and needed me. My mother reminded me that Elisabeth was too old to have a baby. She also reminded me that no virgin had ever given birth before and was not likely to do so now. I kept insisting that I was not dreaming and that an angel sent from God had visited me. Finally, she said that I should go to Judea and see Elizabeth. Was she convinced or did she just yield to my pressure? I did not tell Joseph because my mother insisted that it was not important at this time. This was a hint that she did not believe. However, I did go to see him and tell him that I would be away for a while. It was almost supper time when I arrived at Jacob's house. This would mean my visit would be short. Jacob and Joseph were working on a chair. They were surprised to see me and Joseph offered me a cool drink and a warm smile. I asked to speak to Joseph privately and Jacob excused himself and said it was quitting time. As Joseph looked at me, I felt guilty not being able to tell him what had happened to me that morning. Yet I dreaded having to tell him because he might not believe me either so I told him that my cousin Elizabeth needed me in Judea and I was going to visit her and stay about three months. He really seemed concerned that I would be so far away although we rarely ever saw each other. As we said goodbye, he held my hand and I looked into his eyes and thought of how good it would be for him to hold me in his arms. But would that ever happen? Will Joseph hold a woman who is going to have a baby? Only God knows. I must have faith in God as did Abraham Our Father

A caravan was leaving for Judah the next day and my father had made arrangements for me to travel with them. Elizabeth was overjoyed to see me and she said her baby jumped for joy when she heard my voice. After we had both worshipped the Lord, we had a long talk. She told me about Zacharias' vision and about their baby. God had already told her that I was giving birth to Israel's Messiah. Her talks convinced me that everything was going to be all right. I stayed until John was born and was named it seems strange that my cousin Zacharias started to talk as soon as the baby was named.

Then when I returned home, I conferred with my mother and father about what to do concerning Joseph. We all agreed to go visit and tell them what had happened to me.

We went early in the morning and found them ready for the day's labor. My father began by saying he was glad we were such good friends. Immediately I could see a suspicious look on Jacobs's face. Father also said he was proud to have Joseph as a son. I could see my mother wringing her hands and looking very uneasy. Suddenly she blurted out Mary is going to have a baby! Everyone there was speechless. Finally, Joseph said, "Whose baby are you having Mary?" Then I explained what had happened to me. The whole family tried to be polite to us but must get to work. We would talk again later when we had time to think about it. A few days later Joseph came to our house he sure had a puzzled look on his face he said he wanted to talk to me. We walked outside while my mother was doing the dishes. Joseph said he had been thinking of giving me a bill of divorce in private so as to not cause any more shame on me and my family. His family also agreed that this was the way to handle the situation.

Then he asked me what I was going to name the baby. I told him Jesus was the name the angel of the Lord had given me. A smile came over his face as he told me that God had spoken to him in a dream and also told him to name the baby Jesus for, he shall save his people from their sins. He said he wanted me to be his wife and come and live with him because he loved me. He said he would not doubt my word anymore. Oh, how great is my God for choosing such a wonderful man to be my husband and to be a father to the son of God? Praise the Lord.

Chapter 4

JOSEPH, HUSBAND OF MARY
THE ADVENTURES OF JOSEPH AND MARY

Luke 2

Mary and I had just settled into our little place in our workshop. She sure had it homey looking. Then we were informed that we must go to Bethlehem for the census. I tried to get her to stay home while I went alone but she was of the heritage of David also. So, she started quoting scripture to me. "But thou Bethlehem Ephrathah though thou be little among the thousands of Judah, yet out of thee shall he come forth unto me that is to be ruler in Israel! Who's going forth have been from of old, from everlasting." I recognized that it was from the book of Micah chapter 5, in verse 12. She seemed to think about things that never crossed my mind. We had to travel about 80 miles to Bethlehem which meant we had to make camp along the way. This would give us an opportunity to get to know each other. I still have the written contract our fathers had made when we were betrothed. Since we had not had a formal or religious ceremony, we discussed having one after the baby was born. However, Mary had convinced me that she must remain a virgin until the birth of the Messiah so that the prophecy might be fulfilled. The roads were crowded all along the way. The strangers were very kind to us. We ate with two named David and Ester on the second night. They were older than we were and made us feel most welcome. The third night after we had eaten and were comfortable Mary started telling me that Caesar Augustus was just a tool in the hand of the Lord God. She said he caused us to go to Bethlehem only because God was using him to bring about his purpose. She convinced me that she was right. I guess she will never cease to amaze me.

The fourth night we started planning on where we would stay until the baby was born. We could tell that the time wasn't far off. Since the roads were full of people, we also expected the town to be full. However, Mary was so optimistic, that she said that God would provide a really unique place. I was also excited to see just how he would provide for us. In my mind, I could see a place fit for a king. I went right to sleep as one happy man that night. We hope to make it to Bethlehem today so we were up early and on the road by first light. We really had a good time. We were just outside of town when she decided to walk the rest of the way. We could see a lot of confusion because all the rooms were taken at the inn. I went in to talk to The Innkeeper about a room but he said there was nothing. I inquired about any other place where we might find lodging but he shook his head sadly. I suppose he had answered this question a lot recently.

I went back to talk to Mary and try to make some plans. She said we could camp like we had along the way. Now where could we go? We wanted to have a little privacy. Had not Mary quoted From the Psalms last night? "I will lift up my eyes unto the mountains from whence shall my help come? My help comes from the Lord who made heaven and earth." That was it, we would go up on the mountain. Mary readily agreed and we were on our way. We had just left the crowded streets when we met a man and I asked him if he knew where we could camp for a few nights. He said there was a little cave just at the foot of the hill that was clean and had clean hay.

We could stay there until we could find better quarters. The place was out of the wind and had the smell of fresh hay and there was room for our donkey. We would be better off than most people who came to Bethlehem today. Mary started getting a meal ready and I started getting the donkey fed and preparing a place to sleep when we heard voices and looked to see David and Esther with whom we had eaten the second night on the road. They were going to spend the night here also. Mary invited them to eat with us. What a good meal we had with lots of laughter and joy at having been together again. We sure enjoyed each other's company.

After the meal, we started talking about our common ancestor David king of Israel. Esther loves him for his great kindness. David loves to talk about him being a warrior. I had to tell all of his great humility especially when King Saul was seeking his life. He was also a good friend of Saul's son Jonathan. Mary loved him for the comfort she received from the Psalms. Then she started quoting one. We all joined her because it was so familiar to us. "Shout joyfully to the Lord all the earth. Serve the Lord with gladness. Come before him with joyful singing; know that the Lord himself is God. It is he who made us and not we ourselves. We are his people and the sheep of his pasture." David thought we were the sheep of his stable, everyone was laughing when Mary moaned and grabbed her stomach. We weren't sure they were labor pains for about 10 minutes when she had another. Esther sure was a lot of help since she had delivered babies before and instantly started directing David and me as to what needed to be done. We had everything done that she told us to do and still nothing much had happened.

Mary was quoting another Psalm. "Hear my prayer oh Lord and let my cry for help come to thee. Do not hide thy face from me in the day of my distress. Incline your ear to me on the day when I call answer me quickly." It was just after midnight when the baby came. Mary had had a hard time but she looked so happy. David had fallen asleep and Esther wanted to wake him but I wouldn't have it. I persuaded her to get some rest also. Mary and I had a few minutes to look at baby Jesus and talked for a while. She reminded me of what a great man I was to be trusted to raise the son of God. The very thought of that just overwhelmed me I loved him immediately. Just before I went to sleep Mary said, "Joseph! Didn't I tell you that our God would provide a really unique place for us?"

Chapter 5

SIMON THE SHEPHERD

THE STORY OF THE GOOD SHEPHERD

Luke 2:8—20

There were seven of us shepherds out watching our master's sheep that night. Abner and I were on duty when the angel of the Lord came upon us. The glory of the Lord was so bright that it looked like the sun had suddenly fallen from the sky and was standing just a few feet from us. Abner and I were screaming and our sleepy helpers jumped to their feet they were saying, "Simon! Abner! What is happening?" We couldn't explain it because we didn't know. All I knew was I dropped to my knees and started praying, a practice I had not been doing lately. I was so afraid I don't suppose my legs would have held me up anyway. The light was too bright to look at but I thought I saw a figure of a man or angel.

Then a voice said, "Don't be afraid, behold I bring you good tidings of great joy which shall be to all people. For unto you is born this day in the city of David a Savior, which is Christ the Lord. And this shall be a sign unto you. You will find a baby wrapped in swaddling clothes lying in a manger." Suddenly there was with the angel a multitude of angels praising God. They were saying, "Glory to God in the highest and peace goodwill toward men." They left just as quickly as they appeared. We couldn't see a thing for a while. Finally, our eyes adjusted and I still didn't know what to say. Abner broke the silence by asking me if those were angels. I told him I thought they were because they were praising God for sending a savior which is Christ the Lord. One of the other men thought we should be praising God for sending a savior after all we were the ones in bondage to Rome.

Abner reminded us that the good news of great joy was for all people. I suggested that we should go to Bethlehem and see our savior which God had revealed to us. Then we hurried off looking for the newborn baby wrapped in clothes and lying in a Manger. We saw a light coming from a cave just at the edge of town and knew this was used as a stable, so we stopped to ask for information on the baby. We found some sleepy people who were excited to hear our story. In fact, they knew just what we were talking about. They showed us their baby wrapped in strips of cloth and lying in a manger. We now had great boldness because we had seen our Savior. The city of David was mostly asleep with his ancestors who had come in to register for the census. They were surprised to see shepherd's walking through town telling everybody about a savior who had been born in a stable. We returned to the flock we had left but were different people than the ones who left the flock just a few hours earlier. We were glorifying and praising God for choosing us to witness this great event. We couldn't rest until we had recited the shepherd's psalm together, Psalm 23:

"The Lord is my shepherd; I shall not want. He makes me lie down in green pastures. He leads me beside the still waters. He restores my soul. He leads me in the paths of righteousness for his name's sake. Even though I walk through the valley of the shadow of death I will fear no evil for thou art with

me. Thy rod and thy staff they comfort me. Thou dost prepare a table before me in the presence of mine enemies. Thou hast anointed my head with oil. My cup runneth over. Surely goodness and mercy shall follow me all the days of my life and I will dwell in the house of the Lord forever." Psalm 23 KJV.

Chapter 6

ZACHARIAS

THE ADVENTURES OF TWO BABIES

Luke 2:21–38

Elizabeth had been right when she told me we should not go to Bethlehem for the first three weeks of the month so she could register for taxes. As we rode into town, we could see it was not crowded. It was mid-morning and had no trouble registering. Our plans were to eat lunch and return home before dark. She was homesick for our son John even before we were out of sight of the house. John was almost four months old now and I enjoyed his company as much as Elizabeth but I would never let her know that. Being a priest for God had been more than anyone could imagine, but being a father was something men had been doing for thousands of years. And right now, I was probably happier than I had been in my entire life.

Elizabeth brought me out of my daydreaming and back to reality with an excited voice. "Zacharias! Zacharias! Did you hear the good news? A Savior has been born. We must find Mary and Joseph." I asked her what she had heard. She began telling me that angels had appeared to shepherds out tending sheep. They would find a baby wrapped in swaddling clothes and lying in a manger. They found Mary and Joseph and the baby in a stable at the edge of town. He was wrapped in strips of cloth and lying in a manger just as the angels had told them. We started asking people on the street if they knew a carpenter named Joseph. After a while, we found one who knew where they lived.

We tied our horses in front of the little house and knocked on the door. Mary answered almost immediately. She screamed with delight when she saw Elizabeth. She led us straight into the room to see the baby. He was just lying there and Elizabeth just had to pick him up and start her baby talk. She had had a lot of practice lately. We asked where Joseph was and learned he was at work. As we visited, I reminded Mary that she should go to Jerusalem to present a burnt offering for her cleansing according to the Law of Moses. She said that was almost two weeks away. Naturally, we invited her and Joseph and the baby named Jesus, to stay with us when they came to Jerusalem. Joseph came home for lunch and we ate with them and made some more plans for their trip to Jerusalem. He indicated he wanted to stay here in Bethlehem because someone might say something about Mary. He did have one problem he and Mary had not had a marriage ceremony and they had not been man and wife. They would start sleeping in the same bed after Mary had presented a burnt offering for her cleansing. Then I suggested that we have the marriage ceremony in my house on the day of the burnt offering. We talked this over with the women and they thought it was a wonderful idea and Elizabeth began making plans. We had to leave this excited young couple and return home but not before Elizabeth had made me hold the young baby Jesus. She said not everyone was as privileged as we were to be able to hold the Son of God and our arms. "Did you ever get talked to death? Why do women talk so much about babies or weddings?" Elizabeth had the wedding all planned right down to taking care of the baby Jesus.

Needless to say, I was really glad to get home. Maybe now my ear would get some needed rest. But as soon as she picked up John, she told him the whole story about our trip and the plans for the wedding ceremony. You know, he really seemed interested. You know I really loved it too. Praise God for women. Did you ever hear this little poem said about women?

God created heaven and earth from nothing.

He made all things large and small.

God made man from the dust of the earth.

He made woman last of all.

His heaven and earth are tremendous.

So are his things large and small.

The man he made is stupendous.

But the woman is best of all.

Chapter 7

MARY, PART 2

THE WEDDING

Luke 22:21–38

Joseph and I had been making plans for our trip to Jerusalem to redeem Jesus, my firstborn son. We were up early and had a donkey loaded when the sun came up in Bethlehem. What a day this will be for us, one that we will never forget. We were to bring the Lord of the temple to the temple of the Lord. Since I had not left the house for 40 days, I was like a young child who was finally let out to play. We made Jerusalem in record time and Joseph gave me the price of two pigeons or turtle doves which I dropped into the trumpet-shaped collection boxes in the court of the women. The temple ministrant arranged us women who had presented ourselves in designated places where we could see the cloud of incense, a symbol of our prayers, rise from the altar.

Now that we had been restored to fellowship with our family and community, we could participate in the Redemption of our son for the priesthood. The price was five shekels (about $4.00). For this ceremony, Joseph chose Simeon who was a righteous and devout man. He was so kind and considerate to us. He just had to hold Jesus in his arms. When he held Jesus, he began blessing God, for he knew he was now holding his salvation and the salvation of the whole world. Simeon was definitely filled with the power of the Holy Spirit as he continued to tell us all about the future.

He said Jesus had been prepared before all the people. The Savior was now presented to the world. He said this child was destined for the rise and fall of many in Israel. Those who received him would rise with him, but those who rejected him would fall under his curse. He also indicated Israel would reject their Messiah. He said a sword would pierce my own soul. I thought of how much I love my son. I wondered if God would permit him to suffer such rejection and humiliation.

There was an old prophetess named Anna who had been serving God and a temple for 84 years. Her husband had died after seven years of marriage and she had no children so she gave herself totally to fasting and praying in the temple. She heard Simeon tell him that Jesus was the promised one. She came in and prayed with us and gave thanks to the Lord. Immediately she started telling everyone she saw that our Messiah had come. They were all astonished to see a baby. We were getting a little apprehensive because a large crowd of people had gathered around. Simeon took Jesus into another room and we followed. He had noticed how uncomfortable we were in the crowd and advised us to go out another way. We made our way out of Jerusalem into the Hill Country to the house of Zacharias and Elizabeth thinking we could rest a while.

We were in for a shock because of all the people there from Nazareth. My mother and Joseph's mother were waiting with open arms for Jesus. Elizabeth had the house all decorated for the wedding. The men had made ready a guest house for Joseph and me but we weren't allowed to see it until the ceremony. The plans had all been made for which we were glad. Elizabeth had to make a few alterations to my wedding garment. That afternoon I went to the place my father had rented and waited for Joseph. It was dark when I saw the torches and a small group of people coming toward our place. Joseph was leading the way and their group was noisy. He looked so handsome in the torchlight as he came up to the house and announced that he had come for his bride, and gave my father money. We made our way back to Zacharias' house through the small village with lots of shouts and laughter as we gained more people on the return trip. My heart was just bursting with pride! I was so excited and so relieved that our relatives had believed our story about our baby. We were led to the beautiful little guest house as the rest of the party went into Zacharias and Elizabeth's house for the wedding feast. We found food and drink in abundance in our little hideaway, but most of all we found the great and tender love that only two people can experience when they know the Living God.

Chapter 8

JOSEPH, HUSBAND OF MARY

THE LOST SON

Luke 2:39–52

Our baby has grown from infancy to childhood. Mary had been teaching him about the law and the prophets. He was also being taught in the synagogue in Nazareth. He seemed to be filled with wisdom. I could see that the grace of our God was upon him. Since she loves to quote the scriptures, Mary taught him also. I was amazed at how quickly he learned to quote them. I also taught him how to do carpenter work for he was growing mighty fast. He sure was a rugged child and had a strong spirit. It seemed like only yesterday that he was born, yet he was now twelve years old and we had to go to Jerusalem and present him in the temple as a son of the law. He would then be expected to attend the festivities in Jerusalem as the law prescribed.

Since it was time for the Feast of the Passover, we would make just one trip. We would keep the Passover and the Feast of Unleavened Bread, and then have the ceremony for our son. Our trip to Jerusalem was without incident. We were tired because her family had grown from one to four with another one on the way. But the trip always reminded me of Mary and our first trip to Bethlehem. Oh, how I love that woman, she made a long trip seem like a holiday.

Everything went smoothly for the Passover feast we shared a lamb with another small family, but I must admit I was a little tired of unleavened bread after a week. Even the children were tired of it also. We presented the young man to the priest for the special ceremony there were others there for the same ceremony. One family named Simon Iscariot had a son named Judas who went for the same ceremony. Our son and Judas seemed to have so much to talk about. They were from Kerioth south of Judah and were staying in Jerusalem for a few more days because he was a businessman and wanted to teach his son some things about business in the city.

We said our goodbyes to our new friends and started for home right after the midday meal. We would only go as far as Emmaus today for that is where we would meet our caravan going back to Galilee. After I had set up our tent and had a fire for cooking, I visited a few friends to talk about our eight days in Jerusalem. It was almost dark when I returned for the evening meal. Everyone was there but Jesus. I asked Mary where he was and she thought he was with the men because he had had his ceremony. I thought he was with the women and children because that was whom he traveled with on our way to Jerusalem. After inquiring among our kin folk and acquaintances and did not find him we decided to return to Jerusalem.

We had looked for three days when we met Simon and Judas in the marketplace. They were not surprised to see us because they knew where Jesus was. They were more excited than we were. They kept telling us how he was asking all these different questions of the doctors of the law. When they could not answer he would say, "Have you not read," and then tell them what the Scriptures said. They were amazed at his understanding and the answers he gave.

When he saw us, he came to us and his mother asked him why he had done us this way, I shall never forget his strange answer. He said, "How is it that ye sought me? Knew ye not that I must be about my father's business?" At first, I thought he was talking about my carpenter's business, but he knew we had all the work we could do in Nazareth. After thinking about it I decided that he was talking about the God of Israel. Had not an angel of the Lord appeared to me and told me to name the baby Jesus, for He shall save his people from their sins." And had not the prophets said, "He would be called Emmanuel which means God with us?" I looked at the young man long and hard and for the first time, I could see he was fully aware of who he was, what his relationship to the father was, and what his mission was. Yet he was obedient to his mother and me. I wondered just how I would live with him now that I was aware of who he really was.

Chapter 9

MATTHEW

JOHN THE BAPTIST THE STRANGE-LOOKING MAN

Luke 3:1–22

That was such political turmoil in Jerusalem that many people were confused. For instance, Annas was a high priest because it was his office by birth. However, the Roman government had some problems with him so they took him out of office and appointed his son-in-law Caiaphas as high priest. He could take orders better. His father-in-law Annas still considered himself a high priest so he had a lot of influence on what Caiaphas did. The Sanhedrin was divided over this. The Sadducees believe that they should be subject to what the authorities did because God had put the authorities in charge. The Pharisees said this was completely wrong because men were trying to change what God had told them to do. They also stressed that God's people were to be completely separate from all others and that the sons of Abraham were holy people and heirs to all the promises God made to Abraham.

Still, another group called the Scribes stressed the importance of the traditions of the elders and sided with the Pharisees on the issue of high priests. However Roman flags were flown over the city of Jerusalem signifying the Roman power. Roman soldiers were everywhere to keep the peace. The taxes were collected and sent to Rome causing more irritation among the people. Violence was so common that people traveled in groups even in this city. The robbery was not uncommon. People were insulted and when they rebelled, they were beaten by Roman soldiers without trial.

We started hearing stories about a strange-looking prophet who was preaching in the wilderness area of the Dead Sea. Then he moved up the Jordan and caused a lot of excitement. When I heard he was near I decided to go see him. I learned he was the son of Zacharias and Elizabeth. He was of the priestly tribe. Now that he was 30 years old and ready to take his place with the priests he refused to do so. He was on the banks of the Jordan when I first saw him. I could hardly believe my eyes. First, I had trouble seeing his face because of all the hair he had. His beard was also long and untrimmed. Those clothes he was wearing looked like he slept in them. They were made of camel's hair and he had a leather belt around him. Some said he lived off the land because he only ate what was available. His diet was Locust and wild honey. He could have lived much better if he had joined the priesthood, even though most people did not tithe anymore. On this particular day, many people were there crowding around to hear him. He seemed to be calling the people out of the established religion to repent of their sins and turn back to God. Yet the people were so very attentive to his words.

There were other tax collectors there besides me, along with Gentiles, Samaritans, Roman soldiers, and policemen. John started naming specific sins that most of us were guilty of also laying down certain broad principles of reform. He called for reform and charity giving, food, and clothing to those in need, he pointed out that the established religion was neglecting the poor and using the money for themselves. Publicans were not to exceed the established tariffs. The police officers were instructed to quit handling people so roughly and stop bullying them and taking money from them as bribes for false accusations. Soldiers were told not to complain about their wages.

John was so clear in his message and advice that we all knew he was right in his accusations of what was happening. Until now no one had dared talk of all that was wrong. When John calls for the people to repent from these things they are eager. He asked them to be baptized in the Jordan River, As a symbol of their repentance and confession of sins. He called for us to live our lives in a way that would show we have a completely new way of living. This mode of baptism was familiar because this was the way the Gentiles became proselytes of the covenant. Many of the tax collectors were baptized in the Jordan River just as John had to ask, and I was one of them. The next time I went out to see him he was preaching about the kingdom of God. He was telling everyone that the Lord was coming. All flesh would see the salvation of God. Some thought John was the Messiah. But John said he was only a voice crying in the wilderness. Others thought John was Elijah because the Scriptures had said Elijah would come before the Lord. The priests and Levites pressed him for answers, asking why he baptized if we were not Christ or Elijah. He said one standing among them whom they did not know, whose shoe latchets he wasn't worthy to lose, would baptize them with fire. But he can only baptize with water. Baptism with fire sounded like judgment to me." Was John, right? Was the Messiah here now?

The next day I went back to hear John again. He was preaching on marriage and said it was not lawful for Herod and Herodias to be married. Surely this man was the boldest I have ever heard. While he was preaching on the evils of divorce John suddenly stopped and said, "Behold the Lamb of God which takes away the sins of the world." I looked and saw a man called Jesus. He was of the tribe of Judah. He asked John to baptize him but John hesitated and finally led him into the Jordan and as Jesus came up out of the water the Holy Spirit descended upon him in the form of a dove. A voice came from Heaven and said, "You are My beloved Son; in You, I am well pleased."

John went on to explain that this was Jesus Christ who was to come into the world. This was the one that he had come to announce. He said, "Jesus must increase but that he must decrease." Herod had John put in prison. Finally, John was put to death. But I shall never forget this great man of God. He sure was popular with a multitude of people. They were all attracted to him because he knew what his job was and did it without any reservation. It's no wonder Jesus said, "There was no greater prophet than John the Baptist."

Chapter 10

MARY, PART 3

MY SON STARTS A MINISTRY

Luke 4:14–41

Jesus finally came home. He had been gone for over 50 days. He looked very gaunt and not too healthy. I wondered where he had been and where he had been eating his meals. Wherever it was, he needed more food. I will see to that very soon. There was talk that he had been down to the Jordan River to see John the Baptist. John the Baptist was the son of Elizabeth and Zacharias. He had also been baptized and had gone into the wilderness northwest of the Dead Sea near Jericho. No one had seen him for almost 40 days after that. He soon returned here to Galilee looking and acting like a completely new person. He was preaching in every synagogue where he was allowed. Some people who were following him around said that he had been performing miracles to prove he was the Son of God. The blind was made to see and the lame were walking.

He was asked to read in our synagogue on the Sabbath. He stood up to read the Scrolls in Isaiah: 61:1–2. "The spirit of the Lord is upon me because he has anointed me to preach the gospel to the poor.

He has sent me to heal the brokenhearted, to proclaim liberty to the captives and recover of sight to the blind to set at liberty those who are oppressed to proclaim the acceptable year of the Lord. Then he closed the book, gave it back to the attendant, and sat down. There was quite like death in our synagogue it was as if no one was breathing and all eyes were fashioned on my son. What was the great expectation? Were they expecting another miracle? He spoke, "Today this scripture is fulfilled in your hearing." Jesus also said surely you will quote this proverb to me: "Physician, heal yourself. Do here in your hometown what you did in Capernaum. I tell you the truth, no prophet is accepted in his hometown".

They were saying he was Joseph's son. He is one of us. He told them how Elijah had not gone to anyone in Israel during the 3 and ½ years of drought because of unbelief. Also, How Elijah healed a Syrian rather than an Israelite because of unbelief. Suddenly the packed house was furious with Jesus. They took him to the edge of town to throw him over a cliff, but somehow, he walked away from them. He came home with us but would only stay the night. He wanted to get back to Capernaum because of its strategic location. It was a beautiful place. About 15,000 people live there, most of them Gentiles. Four roads came together just north of the Sea of Galilee. About 4,000 boats were on the Sea of Galilee. The town of Tiberius was also there named in honor of the reigning emperor.

Surely there were more people there than here in Nazareth. So off he went but not alone. James wanted to spend some time with him because he had heard of all the miracles he had done and wanted to see for himself. He did not as of yet believe Jesus to be Messiah. I was very disappointed that our town of Nazareth had not believed in my son. It's no wonder he wanted to leave, just as the prophets of old had done. It seems to me that God never forces himself on anyone. Then when the Nazarenes want to kill him for telling the truth, he was ready to go to another city. James didn't have to wait long. The very next Sabbath in a synagogue in Capernaum he was the teacher. James says that he talked like he had a lot of authority. He also cast out a demon of a man there. Then Jesus went home with Simon. His mother-in-law was sick with a high fever. Jesus went up to her bed and rebuked the fever and it left her. Amazingly she got out of bed and fed the men who were with him. As more and more people came by with their sick families and friends, he laid his hands on them and healed them all. He also cast out more demons who testified that he was the son of God. He kept this up all night and still more and more people came. But when it was daybreak, he left for a place to be alone. But the people came looking for him and wanted to be with him. He told them that he was to go to other towns also and to preach the good news. James had seen enough to convince him that Jesus was no ordinary man, but he needed more time to think about it. Besides he had a business to run and a family to care for. He had been under the Law so long that he wanted to think it over awhile.

Chapter 11

ZEBEDEE, FATHER OF JAMES AND JOHN,
MY SON'S, FISHERS OF MEN

Luke 5:1–11

I hadn't been fishing for several months. I had just gotten too old to keep up with the other men. My two sons James and John had taken over the fishing business. They had taken on two partners, Simon and his brother Andrew. They would be a good influence on my two sons.

We left our families about dark with the promise of a large catch of fish. Now sometimes we say these things just to encourage ourselves. We knew that when the weather was this hot the fish would not come up to the surface to feed and we would probably go home empty-handed. It had been hot all night long and with no breeze to cool us. In fact, I was feeling as warm as the oranges we had packed for a snack. At about midnight, we pulled our two boats together for lunch. My wife Salome had packed us a delicious lunch. To hollow rolls of bread, one filled with cheese and the other with olives. Then for dessert, we had dried figs boiled in grape molasses. This lunch would give us our strength back. My two sons James and John were eating like they were anxious to get back to work. Simon, Andrew, and I were going a little slower while we talked. By now I realized I should have stayed home and sent a hired servant to help fish. But I miss being around the Sea of Galilee. After all, I had fished it for 30 years and it seemed like an old friend to me.

We rowed back to shore about daybreak with no fish. I was so exhausted that I lay down on the sand to rest while Simon, Andrew James, and John repaired the nets. I woke up with a start because Jesus was coming with a crowd of people following him. I have heard about his miracles from everyone, but as of yet never seen one. Maybe he could give me a little energy. He greeted us and quickly got into the boat and asks Simon to thrust out a little. Then I heard one of his sermons. I had not heard him preach before. Suddenly I was wide awake and forgot about my energy drain. I was so amazed that he could quote the scriptures so well. But I should have known this because his mother knew them better than most and probably taught him. You should have been there to hear his sermon. Most people never moved as to catch his every word. Then he told Simon to go out a little further and throw out his net. Simon Peter protested, "Master we have worked hard all night and caught nothing." Simon being an expert fisherman knew the fish weren't feeding because it was so hot, and also because fish go to the bottom as soon as it is light. So he knew it was fruitless labor to try at this time. He would obey Jesus but without any faith that he would catch anything.

Well, Simon was in for a surprise, when the nets were let down the catch was so large that Peter and Andrew were not able to pull them back in. Simon signals his partners to bring the other boats. They filled both boats so full that they were in danger of sinking. Simon Peter saw a miracle that just astonished him. He learned that Jesus knew more about fishing than anyone. He fell down at Jesus' feet and confessed his sin. We all knew that he was not only a great teacher but a great creator; He would one day reign over his creation. We felt so small just standing in his presence but later on, we realized that our faith in him qualified us to stand in his presence. He invited James, John, Simon, and Andrew, to follow him. He said they would be Fishers of Men. So, they just started following him hungry, Sleepless, tired, just walking away. They left me with all those fish to take care of. I went to call my servants to come and take care of them. They would also have to take over the fishing business for my sons. Then I started thinking what kind of equipment do you need to catch men? Then I wondered if Salome had breakfast ready.

Chapter 12

LEVI THE LEPER

JESUS HAS POWER OVER LEPROSY

Luke 5:1215

My wife Judith set my breakfast down and walked away about ten feet, then I came up to eat it. As I ate, we talked about small things such as the children and anything going on in the neighborhood. My leprosy kept me from touching her or anything else and making it unclean. It was very difficult for me not to embrace my wife and two children. My leprosy began with little white specks on the eyelids and on the palms of my hands. Then it gradually spread over other parts of my body. At first, I prayed that I really didn't have it, but as time went on, I knew for sure that I must separate myself from my home and family. If the authorities learned of my disease, they would burn my house. So, I was sleeping in one of my outbuildings and trying to continue my farming. If the neighbors learned that I had leprosy no one would eat our crops or buy eggs from us.

I haven't thought too much about the plight of lepers before and just thought of them as sinners who had it coming to them for all the wickedness they had done. Our whole society looked at lepers as terrible sinners. The rabbis had taught us leprosy was really chastisement for sins. We were also thought to be unclean. No one knew of a cure for my disease. I ate we talked. Judith said she had been to Tiberius to buy fish. Tiberius was about two miles from our farm and a long walk for a woman alone. I was concerned for her safety, but no crimes had been committed here in a long time. She had seen a group of people standing together and someone speaking to them, but she went on to the fish market to find it almost deserted because they said a young Rabbi was in town and everyone was gathered to hear him. So, on her way home, she stopped to hear what he had to say. He had been preaching that the kingdom of God was at hand. She wasn't quite sure what the kingdom of God was but had to ask some other women about it who said that God was ready to set up his kingdom here on earth. In fact, most likely it would be in Jerusalem. I started to wonder if God would have any lepers in his kingdom or if would he just destroy all of us. We were the greatest sinners. And our condition was proof that we were. However, I couldn't remember any great sin that I had committed. My wife's voice kind of woke me up from daydreaming. I was thinking about the kingdom of God and just how it would be. Would it be just like the kingdom that David had? They say that it was the best of times. She was saying that this was the same Rabbi that had been doing all the healings in Capernaum. We had heard that he healed a person with a fever and she eventually got out of bed and went to work. He had cast out demons from others. He seemed to have great authority over all sicknesses and diseases. I wondered if he could heal a leper. The scriptures tell us that the Prophet Elisha had told the Syrian Naaman to dip in the Jordan River 7 times to be clean. I would gladly dip in the Jordan River if he were to ask me to. I asked Judith if she thought I should go into Tiberius to see this rabbi and see if he would cleanse me from this terrible disease. I wonder just how I would go about approaching him, how would the crowd respond to me walking into their midst? Judith said if I were to go to him then I must be determined that he could heal me and that I would not let anything or anyone stop me. Then she said, "Levi, you have everything to gain and nothing to lose. Go for everything."

Immediately I started for the town I met one person along the way, and I ignored him. I saw the crowd and guessed that the rabbi must be in the midst of them. So, I just waited until I was really close to them and yelled out loudly, "leper, leper." The crowd started scattering and I just ran up to the one they call Jesus and fell down before him and said, "Lord if you are willing you can make me clean. "He stretched out his hand and touched me. He said, "I am willing, be clean now." And immediately I was clean. Only my clothes and hair looked like I still had it but I was pain-free and free from sores. He then instructed me to go to Jerusalem and make an offering for my cleansing just as the Law of Moses had commanded.

I would obey immediately after, I went and told my wife and changed my clothes, had a haircut, and took a bath. Now I no longer look like a leper. I no longer felt like a leper. I had new hope. I actually had new life. It was as if I had just been born again. What will the priest say when I tell them Jesus cleansed me from all leprosy? So off to Jerusalem, I went with my offerings. The two doves were used, first one bird was killed and the blood sprinkled on me. The second bird was dipped in the blood and let go free. Then I had to wash my clothes and shave off my hair. On the 8th day, I had to take a male lamb and some flour and oil to the priest. The priest made an offering for my sin. The whole process took several days and I was anxious to get home. The priests and scribes were questioning me over and over about Jesus and how he healed me. They were continually telling me to give credit to God. I kept insisting that this man was sent from God. When they couldn't get me to change my mind, they decided to send some Pharisees to investigate this man Jesus.

I finally made it home after a couple of weeks and was so very happy to see my wife and two children. They all wanted to know about the cleansing ceremony and how I had to do all that even though I was already clean. I tried to explain that I felt obligated to

Jesus to do what he told me to do. This was also in accordance with the Mosaic Law. I would find this young Rabbi again later. I still wanted to hear him preach. He was doing something the priests were not doing. I could hardly wait to see him but was reminded that the weeds were growing better than my crops. My workload had also grown. It would take me 30 days to catch up. Then I would go over to Capernaum and hear this young man. Oh Lord, I feel like a young man again and I thank Jesus for all he's done for me.

Chapter 13

JOSEPH OF ARIMATHEA

HE TOUCHED ME

Luke 5:16–26

Nicodemus and I were sent to Capernaum to find out about this young Rabbi named Jesus. Nicodemus was so excited and had on a new robe. I felt underdressed because he looked so good. We were to report what we saw back to the council. This all started when a leper named Levi came into the temple, to make an offering because he had been cleansed from leprosy. This man owned a farm in Galilee near Tiberius. He had just walked up to the young Rabbi and said you can cleanse me if you are willing. And Jesus had said that he was willing. Then he just said, be clean, and he was made clean. I know because I was at the temple when he came in to make an offering according to the Law of Moses. Some on the council doubted that Levi had ever had leprosy.

I started to wonder, if God would have only lepers in his kingdom or if would he just destroy all of them. The prophets had healed the sick, couldn't this be one of the prophets? What really made Levi, the leper so sure that this was Israel's Messiah was that he touched him. Then that would make the rabbi Jesus unclean also. I had heard of this rabbi. Nicodemus had gone secretly to meet him at nighttime and told me about him. I did not like Galilee, because it was good farmland, and I was not a farmer. It was said in Jerusalem that if you would be rich, live in Galilee. If you would live Godly, live in Judea. Going to Galilee we went through Berea and Decapolis so we wouldn't have to go through Samaria. We arrived and found comfortable quarters at one of the inns. There were several here because lots of travelers came through here to trade. Some of the wealthy came here because the Sea of Galilee had a cool breeze blowing over it most of the time. We heard that the rabbi would be holding a meeting at the home of a fisherman. Our group made our way there in order to get a good view. We didn't know about the seating arrangements here in Galilee, but in Judea, they would give us the best seats in the house. We asked for directions to the house of Zebedee and soon found it. It was a large house with a flat roof. We were led into a large room and found a seat. The room filled up quickly and we were glad to be there first because there wasn't enough seating for all who came. Soon the young Rabbi came in with four Fishermen. There was hardly any room for them. Some were looking in through the windows and doors.

He greeted us and started his message about the kingdom of God. He spoke with authority but looked like an ordinary man. He seemed to know the law so well for a man his age. It was while he was preaching and we were listening so carefully, for we had to give a report accurately. Then we noticed some specks falling from the roof, and the noise of someone on the roof removing the roof tiles. He just kept on with his message but we were all distracted by the hole opening up in the roof. Finally, the men on the roof let down a man through the roof on a mat right in front of the teacher. This didn't seem to bother Jesus at all. When he saw their faith he told the man on the mat, "Friend your sins are forgiven." Well then everyone in that room heard that statement. The Pharisees sitting next to me said,

"Who is this man who speaks blasphemy? Who can forgive sins but God alone?" There were scribes and teachers and even Sadducees here shaking their heads and talking among themselves.

He raised his hand to quiet us down. He spoke again. He said, "Which is easier to say, your sins are forgiven or get up and walk? So that you may know that the son of man has authority to forgive sins, he said to the man with the mat to get up and take your mat and go home". This man immediately jumped up, rolled up his mat, and walked out praising God. Well, we Pharisees had come to see a miracle and we saw one, or was it two? We were praising God, Pharisees, Sadducees, and Scribes. The other people here with us who were fishermen and farmers were also praising God. I sure had something to report to the Sanhedrin. Some of my friends were afraid, some were puzzled, and still others glorified God. When he came over and laid his hand on me and said," Joseph do you believe what you have seen here tonight?" I answered, "Yes Lord. I believe". He said, "Because you believe today, you will see the greatest miracle on earth when I visit you in your garden." I could still feel the touch of his hand as I wondered what kind of miracle he would perform in my garden. You know I believe he is Israel's Messiah. I wonder if he will set up his kingdom in Jerusalem. I would like to be a part of that kingdom.

Chapter 14

JOSEPH OF ARIMATHEA

FAITH – THE NEW WAY TO PLEASE GOD

Luke 5:27—39

Nicodemus and I were very good friends and agreed on most things concerning this young rabbi. But we were alone. In our company were other members of the Sanhedrin who believed exactly the opposite. We both believed Jesus had forgiven the paralyzed man's sins. He had proven it by commanding the man to walk. Others were saying that the paralyzed man wasn't really paralyzed. We investigated further by finding who the friends were that carried him in and let him down from the roof. They all testified that this man was indeed paralyzed. This settled it for us and so we recorded it for the benefit of the Sanhedrin. However, it wasn't good enough for some of the Sadducees and also some of the more conservative Pharisees.

We would stay longer and try to get more information on this son of man as he liked to call himself. We heard that he had called a tax collector- to be one of his disciples. This needed to be checked out very carefully. Hardly anyone spoke to a tax collector. They were considered to be thieves. Why would he make such a big mistake as this, just when he was beginning to attract large crowds? This tax collector had left everything behind to follow Jesus. His contracts with Rome were worth a lot of money. His name was Levi, later called Matthew. Levi or Matthew was so happy that he gave a big reception at his house for Jesus and invited all the other tax collectors and a few other people to come to meet his new friend.

Our delegation had been invited also. We were surprised to see so many publicans there and wondered if we had made a mistake by coming. Some of our groups were reclining beside his disciples and began grumbling at his disciples and asking questions such as, "Why do you eat and drink with tax collectors and sinners?" Jesus overheard the questions and answered for himself. He told us all that only the sick needed a physician. Those who are well don't need one. He said he had come to call sinners to repentance, and not the righteous. That made perfect sense to me because there sure were a lot of sinners here. But just how was he going to make these people well? Surely, he was talking about being sin-sick. How could he bring all these people up to the level of the Pharisees and scribes? I had to ask him this question just as the meeting was over and we were leaving. I had to have it for my report. He was gracious but to the point. He said, "The righteous are those who are righteous in their own eyes. Those who were tax collectors and sinners already knew they were not righteous. They were willing to believe that he was Israel's Messiah and were freely forgiven of their sins. They were made righteous because of their faith. The Pharisees and scribes thought they were well and didn't need a physician."

Not all of us had been baptized by John the Baptist because we thought we needed no repentance. Jesus had given us something new to think about. He made it clear that the Scribes and the Pharisees were taught that they were righteous but they were not. They were self-righteous and did not have the righteousness of God. The sinners who followed them in faith were made righteous, while the Pharisees who rejected him remained sinners. Nicodemus and I had a long discussion that evening about the truth of this message. He told me of the time he went to see Jesus and was told that he must be born again. Nicodemus also told me that if I believed that Jesus was the Messiah then I had already been born again and that I was a member of God's family. This was really exciting and I wondered if I should put this in my report. We both decided that it would only stir up trouble since most of our party did not believe as we did.

The following day they asked Jesus why the disciples of John fasted and offered prayers. The Pharisees also do the same but; his disciples eat and drink all the time. They said we never see them fast or pray. He explained that it was just like a wedding. The attendants of the bridegroom did not fast as long as the bridegroom was with them. But they would fast one day when the bridegroom would be taken away. He also told us a parable about putting new wine into new wineskins so that it doesn't break the skin. I wasn't really sure what he was talking about. He said new wine in old skins would surely break the skins. The same was said of a new patch on an old garment. When it was washed it would tear the old cloth. Also, it wouldn't look right because the cloth would not match. Jesus did not want to patch up the law of Moses. He explained a new way to get to heaven. It was through believing he was Christ the son of God. This new way did away with the Law of Moses and the sacrificial system. Christ gives us the new wine of the Gospel. This new wine of the gospel must be placed in new wineskins of grace, not into the old one of law. Later on, after his crucifixion, we learned of the great change in the Law. His death on the cross would save all mankind if they would repent of their sins and have faith in Him.

Chapter 15

NICODEMUS

JESUS, THE SABBATH BREAKER

Luke 6:1—16

Joseph and I were settled in at the little inn and living very comfortably, but we had been here almost 30 days and missed our families. We had eaten most of our meals here at the inn, but we had also eaten a lot of meals at houses around the area. We were following Jesus of Nazareth almost everywhere he went. It was our job to report what he did to the Sanhedrin so they could make a judgment on whether he was really Israel's Messiah or an imposter. One particular Sabbath we followed him after he had preached in one of the synagogues. The day had been long and all people following him were hungry. Joseph and I included. His disciples began to pluck grain from a field we were passing and roll it in their hands to get the husk off it and then eat it.

Some in our company began to complain to him that his disciples were breaking the Sabbath because most were rolling it in their hands. This they call threshing. The grain plucking was legal according to our tradition but the threshing was forbidden. Joseph and I understood this law very well because we had been taught this from an early age. It was all right for a hungry man to eat grain from someone else's field if he was hungry. However threshing grain on the Sabbath was against our teaching. Jesus explained that David himself had entered the house of God and he and his men ate the consecrated bread which was set aside for priests alone. Then he said, "The Son of Man is Lord of the Sabbath." I looked at Joseph and he said yes you must report this just as he has said it. Then on another Sabbath, he was teaching in a synagogue and a man had a withered hand. This man was born with a small arm and hand which was almost useless. We were all watching Jesus to see if he would heal on the Sabbath. Some in our group were given a report almost the opposite of what Joseph and I were giving. Jesus knew what we were all thinking and asked the man to get up and come forward. Jesus' question was rhetorical, "was it lawful to do good or evil? Is it lawful to save a life or destroy it?" Then he told the man to stretch out his hand and when he did, it was restored just like the other one. Some of our party was filled with rage because of his healing on the Sabbath. They started asking us what they could do to Jesus for breaking the Sabbath. My advice was that if he was the Messiah as he had said last week, there was nothing that we could do. If he was Lord over the Sabbath, he was Lord over everything else. Actually, I saw nothing wrong with asking a man to stretch out his hand. After all, priests did more work than this every Sabbath. This was not pleasing to the ears of our fellow Pharisees. They accuse Joseph and me of being followers of this imposter. Jesus did something unusual that I thought should be recorded. He went up into the mountain and prayed all night. We were told that he had to make some hard choices and needed God's help. When he came down out of the mountain, he chose from his disciples 12 men. These men were called apostles. How did they differ? All disciples were followers of Jesus of Nazareth. They were also believers. But the apostles had authority that the disciples did not have. They were called the sent ones. They would be with Jesus all the time and in all places. But his disciples would only follow when they could. Their work would hinder them from following all the time. The 12 apostles he chose were Simon Peter and his brother Andrew, James and his brother John, Philip, Bartholomew, Matthew the tax collector, Thomas, James the son of Alpheus, Simon the Zealot, Judas son of James, and Judas Iscariot. These men had authority, we wondered just how much authority they would possess. Would they be able to heal or cast out demons? Opposition to Jesus was growing as fast as his popularity here in Galilee. The poor were flocking to him, but in Judah, there was great opposition. It seemed that they had already made up their mind that he was really an imposter.

After he named His twelve apostles, he did something different. He healed everyone who was there. We were on level ground with a great crowd of people. There were his disciples and his new twelve apostles. Plus, people from Judea and Jerusalem, and from the sea coast of Tyre and Sidon came to hear him and to be healed of their diseases. Many were tormented by evil spirits, and he healed the whole multitude. Something new was that the multitude all wanted to touch him. He said the power went out of him and healed as many as touched him. This all happened before he gave us what is known as the Beatitudes. This was like a free dinner when you could eat all you wanted and take some home for later. Everyone was completely healed. Everyone believed in him. How could they not? The proof was in their body which had been made well. There was rejoicing like never before. Woo Hoo happy day. I wish they were all like this one.

Chapter 16

JOSEPH OF ARIMATHEA
HOW TO OBTAIN RIGHTEOUSNESS

Luke 6:17–49

Jesus had on numerous occasions talked about the kingdom of God. So, he found a level place on the mountain with the 12 by his side talking about the blessedness of being poor, and those who weep. He was separating people as he would sheep from goats. He sure was different from all we had been taught. The shocking thing to us Pharisees was how he kept referring to us, as not really ready for God's Kingdom. He warned the people about the teaching of the Pharisees: saying" Unless your righteousness exceeds that of the scribes and the Pharisees you will not enter the kingdom of God."

We all know that a person must be righteous to enter God's Kingdom. Actually, we have been practicing righteous acts all of our lives. We observed all the ceremonies and all the laws. We had kept all the traditions handed down to us. Just what kind of righteousness was he talking about? How did he have better righteousness than we? We knew what was required by the law. He kept teaching that righteousness good enough for God's kingdom must come by faith in him. Righteousness could not be earned by keeping feasts, rituals, or traditions. Here again, was a great rift between what he taught and what we had been taught. Then he offered himself as the only way to God. His righteousness was not earned but given freely to everyone who believed he was the promised Messiah of Israel. His miracles made it difficult not to believe, but some hated him because he was so popular with the poor and the outcast. Another thing he said was a parable about Two Men Who Built Houses. One was built on a foundation of rock and when the rains fell and the floods came the house stood firm because of its solid foundation. The other man built his house on the ground and when the rains and the wind came the house fell because of a bad foundation. He said, "The person who listened to him and acted on his word was like the man whose house was built on a solid foundation. But the man who hears his words and doesn't do as he says is like the house that had no solid foundation and fell into ruins". For my report to be made plain to my fellow council members I had to once again approach Jesus with some questions concerning righteousness. He seemed to know what I wanted before I asked him.

He explained that to be poor in spirit one must be a beggar in spirit. Meaning he had no good works to show God. He had absolutely nothing to come to God with to earn his way into heaven. The poor in spirit would then be open to receive the true righteousness that God gives to all who trust in his Son. Those who mourn are described as those who recognize they have no righteousness and confess their sins to God. He said mourning and confession were associated together. We Pharisees had been taught that we needed not to mourn because we had kept all the Commandments and done all the laws required. The meekness that God demanded of all those who would enter his kingdom was an attitude of submission to God's authority. Those who submit to his authority would be meek enough to enter his kingdom and he would also inherit the earth. Those who hunger and thirst for righteousness were just like a person who could not quench his thirst for what the Pharisees had to offer. What he needed was to totally rely on God for his righteousness. That meant an appetite for God. Jesus explained that true righteousness was also merciful. We had been taught that we had no responsibility towards the poor, sick, and lonely. These were signs of divine displeasure. God had these folks under his punishment according to our teachings. True righteousness produces mercy care and concern for the needs of others. The sermon he gave on the mountain had been given before so it angered all the Pharisees and Sadducees. He had laws different than what our traditions had taught. Ours was by keeping the law to get into God's Kingdom. His was by belief in God's Son would make all men acceptable in God's kingdom. I believe that Jesus is truly the son of God. I think that I will come into a great Inheritance when I die.

Chapter 17

NICODEMUS

SAVING FAITH

Luke 7:1–17

Joseph and I were glad Jesus had come back to Capernaum. It made it easy for us since we were living in the inn here on the sea of Tiberius. The breeze from the lake was cool but sometimes we had to endure the smell of fish. We had been talking most of the night with the other Pharisees about the sermon on the mountain. The questions were about the good tree and the bad tree. The blind was leading the blind and a man taking a speck out of someone's eye and having a log in his own eye which he couldn't see. The discussion sometimes got Loud and sometimes heated. We tried to keep it quiet for the sake of the other guests, but they were interested also. Just after breakfast, we were waiting to see what Jesus would do today. We knew it would be exciting and make some of us happy and some of us sad. But all were enthusiastic and ready to see what he would do next. A runner came and told Jesus about a Roman Centurion, a man who commanded

100 men, who had a sick servant. The servant was almost dead and no one could save his life. He asked Jesus to come and save his life. The runner said his master was a worthy man. He loved Israel and built a synagogue for them. So, Jesus started toward the centurion's house and was met by some of his friends whom he sent to tell him not to come any further because he wasn't worthy of Jesus to come to visit his house. In fact, he had said he wasn't worthy to come into Jesus' presence, and that was why he sent someone else to get him. He only wanted Jesus to give the command so his servant would be healed. He explained that he knew what it was to give and take orders since he was a military man. All he asked of Jesus was to give the order and his servant would be healed. Jesus turned to all of us who were following him and said, "I have never found this great a faith in Israel." When those who had come to tell Jesus not to come any further returned to the house, they found the servant completely healed and in very good health. I started thinking about saving faith. Did it take as much faith as the Centurion to become a believer? I talked to Joseph about it and we decided that we didn't have to have that kind of faith just to be saved because he'd already said that if we believe that he was the son of God then that was having faith. Then we wondered if we had to have as much faith as a centurion in order to be healed. This was truly a remarkable miracle that had been done and it would be talked over all evening.

The next day It was told to us by his disciples that he was going to the city of Nain. That meant walking about 20 miles a day and finding a place to stay the night. Following this man wasn't easy. He was in tremendous shape from all of his walking. Joseph and I were not the only ones with sore feet and tired legs from long walks. Most of the Pharisees and Sadducees were also out of shape. He wanted to go through Nazareth and everyone got to see his mother and other family members. It was almost noon and Jesus was hungry for some home cooking. Joseph and I had carried our lunch because sometimes he never stopped for food. Others in our group found a place to purchase food, so everyone was fed. We wondered if he would do any work while he was here. But just after he ate, we were all off for the second half of our journey. Sometime in the afternoon, we arrived in the city of Nain. The city was walled, but the gates were open. As we entered through the gates, we were met by a very large crowd of people with a dead person being carried. The mother of the dead person was a widow and was weeping. Then Jesus asked the men to stop so he could get more information. He told the mother not to cry. Then he walked over and touched the coffin and told the young man to get up. The dead boy rose up and began to talk. Jesus helped him from his coffin and gave him to his mother. The entire crowd that was following the casket was filled with awe and began praising God. The crowd that was following Jesus was taken by surprise that he had raised a man from the dead. They were expecting him to hold some kind of meeting before he did anything outstanding. So, our group also began praising God. We had a wonderful time there praising God in a city I had never been to before. The people of Nain thought God had sent a great prophet. There were some in our crowd who thought it was all fake. But a few of us Pharisees believe Jesus to be the son of God. He had been critical of us an awful lot but we were beginning to see his criticism was justified.

When we were fully in the city, he found a place suitable to speak to the townspeople. After his sermon about the kingdom of heaven being at hand, he started healing the sick. Many with diseases were healed. Some who were blind were made to see. He even cast out evil spirits from some people. Truly this had been a most exciting day. The people of this city were out in full force to see this man of God and they were not disappointed.

Some of John's disciples came to see Jesus and wanted to know if he was the expected one or if he had to look for another. Jesus told them to report to John what they had seen that day. Blind receive sight, the lame walk, lepers cleansed, the deaf hear, the dead are raised, and the gospel has been preached to the poor. I think this was the most wonderful day we had ever had with Jesus. He has to be God In the flesh, for no one can do the things he does. How can anyone reject him?

Chapter 18

ANDREW

JESUS HAS DINNER WITH PHARISEES

Luke 7:36—50

Simon a Pharisee of good reputation invited Jesus and his Apostles to his house for an evening meal. He had an elaborate house and looked like the richest man in the city. His robes were of the finest material and his house was larger than any of his neighbors. He must have entertained many people for his table was large enough to accommodate most of his guests. He had other smaller tables in the same room when he had lots of guests. The doors were open and a woman came to see Jesus and knelt at his feet while he was reclining at the table. She was washing his feet with her tears and drying them with her hair. She kept kissing his feet and anointing them with perfume. Simon the Pharisee thought to himself, that if Jesus were truly a prophet of God, he would know that this woman was a sinner and tell her to go away. Jesus not only knew about the woman but also knew what Simon was thinking. He explained to him about Sinners and forgiveness. Those who are great sinners and are forgiven love more than those who have not sinned as much. Then he forgave the woman her sins and all who were in the room with him were amazed, and wondered who he was that he could forgive sins

"Jesus said to the woman your faith has saved you, go in peace." When Jesus justifies the woman in the eyes of Simon, he points to her good works, for only through her works could Simon see the proof of her faith. But when he sent the woman away in peace, He pointed to her faith that saved her, not her works.

We apostles who were on duty had to speak to all the people who came into contact with Jesus. Most of them were baptized before they went home. Some refused baptism and wanted to think about it for a few days. Sometimes we had hundreds to baptize when there was a meeting. This woman was a surprise to us because she walked into a house uninvited. It was our job to talk to her before she left. If she wanted to commit her life to be a follower of Jesus then she was baptized. Since we were by the Sea of Galilee, John and I baptized her there.

When there were hundreds to be baptized then at least ten of us were on hand to see to the needs of the people. We always kept track of how many were baptized, but not the names, however, we always knew which region had the most followers.

Chapter 19

NATHANIEL BARTHOLOMEW
JUDAS, THE FINANCIAL ADVISOR

Luke 8:1—40

There was never an abundance of money. There always seemed to be just enough for the provisions of our group. The money came from merchants, tax collectors, even Romans, and lots of ordinary people. However, there were several people who traveled with us who always saw to our needs, time and again. When I thought we would go hungry these people would give liberally to Judas for he managed all the money and bought all the supplies. Two prominent women were traveling with us and on several occasions contributed greatly to our cause. Joanna the wife of Chuza had heard and believed that Jesus was Christ. Susanna was also wealthy and a good friend of Joanna, and she also saw to our needs more times than I can remember.

We were just about three miles from Capernaum in a small industrious town called Magdala. Jesus was preaching his Kingdom message. A young woman came to him with disheveled hair and eyes that were strange-looking. Jesus saw her problem immediately, for she had seven demons and she seemed to be insane. He immediately cast out the demons and she praised Jesus for what he did for her. She just stayed with us all day. We learned that she was from a wealthy family, who owned a fish Market. They would buy fish and salt cure them and sell them all over Israel. She was so thankful for that that she joined our traveling Ministry. Joanna and Susanna took good care of her. She seemed to fit right into our group for she had a sweet and loving spirit now that Jesus had made her clean. We called her Mary Magdalene. Jesus had made our headquarters here in Capernaum and I was glad that we had rented a house very close to the Sea of Galilee. The breeze from the lake was a real blessing for sometimes the heat was unbearable. I had noticed just how pretty Mary was after Jesus had cast out those seven demons. It seemed that her face wasn't drawn anymore and she had the most beautiful eyes. I wondered if she was married or espoused to someone else. Philip said to me," Why are you staring at the new woman?" I did not know I was staring. I told Philip that she was beautiful and he agreed.

This was also a trade route, and we saw many merchants with Caravans. Judas was interested in trading with these people, mostly Gentiles, who not only had good things to sell but had a lot of money to buy. We were often given objects of value that we had to carry around and that we could not spend. So, when Judas met some Gentiles with lots of money, he would try to sell our wares to them. This sometimes took him away from the 12 and the master while he conducted the business. Sometimes the other eleven would be short with him because he was not there every minute of the day. A lot of time he was late catching up with us because the business was sometimes burdensome. Peter and John had been fishermen and good businessmen, but they were no match for the merchants he had to deal with. Peter was the worst to criticize. John never said too much. Jesus never said anything about him managing our affairs. He and Judas got along just fine. Perhaps it was because he was the only apostle who was not from Galilee, and that made us jealous.

Perhaps we were jealous also because he had known Jesus since he was 12 years old.

This particular day when we got back Jesus was talking about farming. These people knew what farming was all about and I suppose that is why he told us the parable about the Sower and his wheat. I remember he said, "Some fell by the wayside and birds ate it. Some fell on rocks and started to grow but then withered. Some fell among thorns and was choked out. Then some fell on good ground and bore a lot of grain". Then he explains this Parable to us 12. We all wanted to be good soil and bring forth one hundredfold. This was sure a good parable and one I would never forget, although I was not a farmer. I also wondered just what kind of soil I really was.

Jesus had been walking most of the day and standing the rest while teaching. So, he requested that we go across the lake. He was soon asleep, and we were all just letting the sails take us across. However, the wind suddenly became severe and the waves were very high. The boat was heading and pitching so we thought we would drown. John rushed to Jesus and woke him. He said something about us almost drowning. Jesus got up and spoke something to the wind and all of us sudden it quit blowing and the water was as smooth as glass. Then he chided us about our little faith. But we were all marveling that he could talk to the wind and waves and they would obey him. We had seen a great miracle that day but there was more to come.

Just as we were coming to land on the other side of the lake in the land of Gadarenes we saw a man walking about the cliffs where the dead were buried. He was naked and came running toward us. He knew Jesus for he called him by name, and called him the Son of God most high. This man said his name was Legion for that is how many demons we're in him. Could Jesus cast out 6,000 demons at one time? Then the demons started talking to Jesus and begging him not to send them into the deep. Instead, he permitted them to enter a herd of swine that was feeding on the mountain. Jesus had to give them permission to enter the swine and immediately they started running down the hill and over the cliff and into the Sea of Galilee where they drowned.

Someone in our boat had some clothes for the naked man and when the people of the town came out to see what going on, they found Legion was sitting at the feet of Jesus, clothed and in his right mind. Now Legion wanted to go with us because he loved Jesus, but Jesus told him to return to his own house and show what great things God has done for him. Then he went his way and it is told that he told the whole city what great things had happened to him. But there was no rest for Jesus because people were waiting on the shore for our boat to arrive.

Chapter 20

JAIRUS

TWO MIRACLES OF HEALING

Luke 8:41—56

I was by the shore of the Sea of Galilee waiting with a very large crowd of people. We had heard that Jesus had raised the dead in the city of Nain and had healed the servant of a centurion who was a Gentile. I wanted him to heal my daughter who was very sick. I thought she might die if something wasn't done soon.

I was hopeful that Jesus would come to my house and just say the word and my daughter would be healed. It was told to me that he never even went to the house of the Centurion, but only spoke the word, and his servant was healed. This same Centurion was a generous man and had built the synagogue of which I was a ruler. He was a good man for a Gentile but had not become a proselyte. However, he was always giving to the poor, and also given to the support of the synagogue, for he had learned to love Israel.

I had been thinking of all the things Jesus had done and how I would approach him when I saw his boat come to the shore. I was first to greet him and fell down at his feet and begged him to come to my house where my only daughter, who was only twelve years old lay dying.

The crowd was so large that they were pressing against one another. They were not unruly, but we were very anxious to touch the master. Jesus suddenly stopped and said who touched me? And when no one came forward Peter said, "Master look at the great crowd that is pressed up against you and you ask who touched you?" Jesus said that someone had touched him because he felt power go out from him. Suddenly a woman from the crowd came and said that she had touched him because she thought if she could only touch the hem of his garment she could be healed. She had an issue of blood that could not be cured by any Physician and, she had spent all she had and was not yet cured. Now that she had touched him, she was healed immediately. Jesus told her to go in peace for her faith had made her well. He had called her daughter. Had her faith also saved her from her sin? Just then my brother Aaron came and said not to trouble the master because my daughter had died. Jesus said not to fear but only believe and she would be made well. I tried to recall how he had raised the widow's son in Nain and hoped he would do the same for me. So as soon as we arrived the other relatives and friends told him he was too late, that she was dead. But he said she was only sleeping. They mocked him by saying, "Oh yes she's only sleeping," So he put all out except me, her mother, and James and Peter and John. He took her by the hand and said, "Little girl, arise" and her spirit came into her again and she arose immediately. Those were the three most beautiful words I have ever heard, "Little girl arise." My daughter was alive, my wife could not believe it until she gave her a big hug. We were all praising God for the life he had given back to us. Then he told us something very strange. He said that we were not to tell anyone what was done in that room.

What a story to tell in the synagogue. But I am forbidden to tell them. I think he is God.

Chapter 21

PETER

THE POWERFUL TWELVE

Luke 9:10—17

Jesus was ready to send out his 12 Apostles to preach the same message that he had been preaching all over Israel. He had informed us what was happening all around us, and how tough it would be to convince the people here that the kingdom was very near. He told us the Pharisees were teaching us to follow them and their tradition and they would lead us into life. The people were hungry for the truth and the true shepherd. Jesus said there was a great need for more workers for their Harvest was great. So, he called us together and gave us his power and authority. He instructed us to go only to the lost sheep of Israel. We were to preach the kingdom message he and John had preached. We were to perform the same miracles he had performed, such as healing the sick, cleansing the lepers, and preaching the kingdom message. The people who believed our message was to feed us and meet our needs. Their Hospitality would show us they believed our message. We were to stay at the home of respectable people. If we found a village that had no hospitality we were to move on.

We were all surprised by the power he gave us to heal sick people. And we're all pleased that lots of people believed our message. It seemed we were ready to tell our story to anyone who would listen. In fact, Herod the king heard what was happening and was greatly perplexed. He had reports that John the Baptist had risen from the dead, and some said Elijah had appeared. He was so really stirred up and wanted to see the one who could do such things as these.

When we returned and gave an account to Jesus of all we had done, he withdrew and took us to a desert place belonging to Bethsaida. The multitude had been watching us and following us, so he began speaking of the kingdom of God and healing all sick people. They stayed all day and we twelve told him to send the multitude away so we could find food and lodging.

He said first feed them. We replied that we had no way of doing that. There were only five loaves of bread and two fish in this whole crowd and there were about five thousand men in this group plus women and children so he said, "Make them sit down in groups of fifty", and we did so. Then he took the five loaves and two fish, and looking up to heaven he blessed and broke them, and gave them to us. When they all ate and were satisfied, we took up all that was left and had twelve baskets of food left. Oh, what a lesson we learned that day. His miracles authenticated his message. The multitude heard and saw and believed. I wonder why the Jewish leaders were so stubborn and slow to believe him. They were constantly looking for reasons to reject him. Most of their followers follow them because they had been brought up to believe they were their shepherds. Now Christ had revealed them as false shepherds, and they had made up their minds to get rid of him.

I think I neglected to tell you that this all happened around Bethsaida my hometown. Most people call Bethsaida Fish Town. Andrew and I were happy to be home again and see our families. We were glad that we could give Hospitality to our master and our brothers in the faith. We were so happy that Christ had healed so many of our people. This was the largest miracle I had ever seen him perform when he fed so many people. Our families were so glad to see us and cook and clean up after us but there was not a whole lot of privacy which we missed also.

Jesus did not waste any time in getting started north towards Mount Herman and Caesarea Philippi. It was there that he asked the question, who do the people say that the son of man is? We had heard people say John the Baptist, others said Elijah, and others said, Jeremiah. Then he asked, "Whom do you say that I am?" I answered, "You are the Christ of God." He told us not to say anything about this because he must suffer many things. The four things he told us he must go to Jerusalem the only place for a sacrifice. I was puzzled by this because he had never sacrificed before. I wondered what kind of sacrifice he would make. Then he said he must suffer many things from the chief priests, the elders, the teachers of the law, and all the religious leaders of the nation. Then he said he must be killed but would be resurrected on the third day. Since I felt I was a leader and spokesman of our group, I spoke up boldly. I first pulled him aside and told him that this shall not happen to him. I was thinking we could stay away from Jerusalem. We had too many enemies there. He turned on me quickly and said, "Get behind me Satan; you are an offense to me, for you are not mindful of the things of God, but the things of man." I was ready to use physical force on him to protect him. Now after looking back at, it, I can see that Satan was really using me to prevent Christ from doing the will of the Father. After thinking and praying about it for a long time I can see that I was not mindful of the things of God. I was only thinking of saving his life. I find that I'm not much of a leader. It's just like he said, when the blind lead the blind they will all fall into a ditch. Lord God, please give me understanding and help me to be a leader.

Chapter 22

PHILIP

HOW ABOUT ETERNAL LIFE?

Luke 10:25—37

Jesus was being tested by an expert in the law. He wanted to know what he had to do to inherit eternal life. Jesus asked him what was written in the law. And the man said," You shall love the Lord your God with all your heart, with all your soul, and with all your strength, and with your entire mind, and your neighbor as yourself." Jesus told him he had answered correctly. Then he asked Jesus who his neighbor was. Jesus already had a wonderful story to tell the man that would clarify it for him. I was glad when he had a story because I didn't understand what he was trying to say.

I usually had Nathaniel who was quick to catch it the first time. I was born and raised in Bethsaida the city of Andrew and Peter but I had a real burden for all my relatives who were Jewish in practice, but we also had Greek names. My parents named me after Philip the tetrarch of Galilee at the time of my birth. With that Gentile name, you would think that I would catch it as fast as Nathaniel but not so. I had to think about it over several days.

Now back to our story after all my ramblings. The lawyer wanted to know who his neighbor was, and Jesus talked about a person who left Jerusalem and went down to Jericho and fell into the hands of robbers. He was left beside the road and beaten, robbed, and naked. He needed real help badly. A priest passed by him but offered no help. Then a Levite passed by and gave no help. Then a Samaritan who was despised by Jews came down the same road. He saw the needy man and decided to help him. He cleaned his wounds with wine and soothed them with oil, bandaged him, put him on his donkey, and transported him to an inn. He stayed the night and saw the man was better. He paid the innkeeper for help and gave him money to take care of him until he was well enough to travel. Then Lord Jesus Christ asks the law expert who was this man's neighbor. The expert only had one answer, the man who had mercy on him. Jesus told the man to do the same thing.

I heard the familiar voice of Nathaniel coming and said Clippity-clop clippity-clop. He was playing on my Greek name which means lover of horses. You must know that I was the first called disciple and I followed him. He called me and I was ready. Now Andrew and Peter were the first to come to Christ, they had returned to their trade and about a year later they were called to discipleship. Meanwhile, you have heard about Andrew finding Simon, Philip found Nathaniel. I have a great burden for my people in Bethsaida and I always had help from my good friend Nathaniel. He is quick to give an answer. Andrew and Simon were from the same town and were the ones who told me that they had found Israel's Messiah. Then I went searching for him and he found me and called me and I will never be the same.

Luke 11:1–13

One day Jesus prayed and we listened, then I asked him to teach us to pray just as John taught his disciples. This is what he said, "When you pray say,

'Our Father in Heaven, Hallowed be thy name. your kingdom comes your will be done on Earth as it is in heaven. Give us day by day our daily bread. And forgive us our sins, for we also forgive everyone who is indebted to us. And do not lead us into temptation. But deliver us from the evil one.'"

Then he taught us further of which I am glad. He said a man went to his neighbor to borrow three loaves of bread. It was late night and the neighbor was in bed and said no. But this man insisted and said, I have some friends who have come a long way and I have nothing to give them. So, he kept knocking and he finally got up and gave him what he wanted. Then Jesus said, "Ask and it shall be given to you. Seek and you shall find. Knock and it shall be open to you. For everyone who asks receives. And he who seeks finds, and to him who knocks, it shall be opened. If a son asks for a fish, will you give him a snake? Or if he asks for an egg, will you give him a scorpion? If you being evil know how to give good gifts to your children, how much more shall your heavenly Father give the Holy Spirit to those who ask him?" Now I bet you can guess who I talked to after this story.

I said to Nathaniel, "That was not a lot of training, I didn't get it." Nathaniel said that what He told us was an example for us to follow. Let me explain further. First address God as father. That shows that we as children are dependent on the father. That's attitude. The acceptable prayer also includes worship. That is included when we say Hallowed be your name. Your kingdom come shows we are interested in God's Kingdom, and his work. We are to pray for our daily food and thank him when we get it. Then we are to confess our sins and ask for forgiveness. We should pray for protection and to be led to places where we will not be tempted. It seems to me that God is telling us that he delights to hear our prayers and to keep on praying until he gives us what we ask for, or according to our needs. Then we are to keep asking, keep knocking until the door is open. I also think he will respond to our needs. Not our wants. The last thing he says he will give us is His Holy Spirit. Now I don't know much about the Holy Spirit but I am willing to learn as he teaches us.

Well, now you can see why I travel with Nathaniel beside me when I can. That is why when the Greeks came to me and said we would see Jesus I called my companion Nathaniel, and we took them to Jesus. He always knows what to do. I shall pray for him tonight and then I will pray with more boldness now that I know how.

Nathanael seemed to have his mind on something else lately. I asked him about it and he simply said nothing. But even then, I didn't think he was listening. Then he asked me if I had seen Mary Magdalene today. I told him that she had gone home for the weekend and I thought he should go home also since he had his mind on her all the time. He turned a little red in the face and grinned.

Chapter 23

NICODEMUS

A HOUSE DIVIDED CANNOT STAND

Luke 11:14—36

Joseph and I had been in Jerusalem visiting our families. Then we were told to go back and follow the Galilean and report what he was doing. We were welcomed by most of his followers and they were interested in knowing just what the Sanhedrin thought about our report. We told them that the Sanhedrin wasn't too vocal about it, and they would discuss it more now that we weren't there. Phillip told us we had missed the lecture Jesus gave on prayer. Peter told us that Jesus had given the 12 apostles power to witness, heal diseases, and cure lepers.

We wanted to know what the schedule would be tomorrow. No one seemed to know. We were up bright and early the next morning and found Jesus alone. He asked us what happened in Jerusalem. We were more than happy to tell him that he was not popular there and that he should not go there because it was too dangerous. Soon his disciples began coming in to hear us talk and then others saw a crowd. So, he decided to give a lecture. Two men came by and wanted healing for a dumb man. I think he was unable to speak for the last year. Jesus cast the demons out of the person and suddenly he spoke, and all new people marveled at what had been done. Someone in the crowd said that he was cast out of demons by Beelzebub ruler of demons. Then others sought a sigh from heaven. The first group was saying that Jesus was possessed by Satan. Jesus spoke and told them that if he and Satan were working together to cast out demons Satan's kingdom would collapse. He said that would be like his kingdom was at war with each other. Then he said, "If I cast out demons by Beelzebub by whom do your sons cast out demons? Let them be your judge. But if I cast out demons by the finger of God, then the kingdom of God has come upon you." What he was saying was that they must make a choice. He is also saying we are for him or we are against him. Then he said we are either gathering or we are scattering. Joseph said to me," he sure is laying it on the line today. People are for him or against him. He has already said he came down from the Father. What he is really saying is if we miss heaven, then this life is wasted". I had to say "Amen to that." I thought of all the people here today listening to the Son of God and will not go to heaven. They simply did not believe his story.

He continued with his lecture by telling of a man, who had an unclean spirit, and when it was cast out the unclean spirit wandered around seeking a resting place but he didn't find any. Then he goes back to the person he lived in before and takes up residence there, for he finds his former home swept nice and clean. Then he goes and finds seven other spirits that are eviler than he is and the state of the man is worse than it was before.

Joseph said to me let's talk to Nathaniel about who this man is. We found Nathaniel with his friend Philip and Philip was just asking for some guidance on what was said. So, we listened for a while until we could ask him who was the man who had an unclean spirit cast out and then it came back with seven more companions and left the person worse off than he was before. Nathaniel said he thought Jesus was talking about Israel. Israel had been cleansed by the preaching of John the Baptist, and then he was killed. So, all of Israel did not receive their Messiah and would probably kill him also. Now they are more wicked and guilty than they were before. He went on to say that he thought we may all be in danger from the powers in Jerusalem. We had to agree that no followers of Jesus would be welcome in the temple, and maybe we would be wise to try to keep Jesus away. Then we went back to hear Jesus again just, as a woman from the crowd raised her voice and said, "Blessed is the mother who bore you and nursed you." Jesus responded by saying, 'Yes but better still, blessed are those who listen to God's message and practice it." He began to tell how wicked this generation really is. This is exactly what Nathaniel had just said about how bad it is getting to be. The people wanted a sign from heaven. He said there would be a sign and it was the sign of Jonah. He said that Jonah had been a sign to the Ninevites. So, the son of man will be a sign to Israel. The Ninevites would be a witness against this generation at the judgment because they repented at the preaching of Jonah, and behold someone greater than Jonah is here.

Just as the meeting was breaking up one of the Pharisees asked Jesus if he would have lunch with him. He went into his house and we waited around for a while and then went to lunch ourselves. The next morning, we went to where he was staying, and behold, he was also up earlier than all his disciples. We were glad for we wanted to know how the lunch with the Pharisees went. We noted he had been really hard on them in his speech yesterday. I should say he was hard on us yesterday because Joseph and I were Pharisees ourselves, and we were members of the Sanhedrin. He did not comment on it at all. So, we had an opportunity to find out about the table talk. He smiled as he started telling us about the wonderful things he had to eat. Then he became very serious about the talk. They had called to his attention then he had not washed before the meal. So, he criticized them by telling them that they were just like the dishes we were served in. The cup and the platter were washed on the outside and looked good to everyone. They had forgotten about the inside.

You Pharisees or just like the dishes. You look good on the outside but inside you are full of robbery and wickedness. You people are foolish because when God made you, he wanted you clean on the outside and also on the inside. Give what is inside the dish to the poor and everything will be clean for you. Then he said woe to you Pharisees because you tithe all your garden herbs but neglect love and justice. You should practice the love of God and you will have it right. Then he said, "God condemns the Pharisees because of their pride. They love to be seen in the marketplace and the chief seats in the synagogues." He also compared them to unmarked graves which defile a person who steps on them.

Jesus answered and said, "Woe to you because you load people down with burdens that or hard to bear and you will not lift a finger to help them." Then Jesus said, "Come to me you who are burdened and heavily laden and I will give you rest. Take my yoke upon you and learn from me, for I am gentle and humble in heart and you shall find rest for your souls. For my yoke is easy and my burden is light."

He said we had hidden the truth. We had taken the key of knowledge from the people. He said we had not entered into God's Kingdom and were hindering those who were entering. Jesus said he had come as a light but the Pharisees had bound men in darkness. The Pharisees and lawyers were so angry that they started to bombard him with questions and tried to catch him by something he might say.

It was just Jesus, Joseph, and I when we started talking with him but they kept coming until we were crowded and couldn't move. We had heard a lot of table talk and we had not had breakfast yet.

We finally made our way through the crowd and into the inn which was mostly empty because everyone was outside listening to Jesus. We saw two people sitting over in the corner as if they did not want to be disturbed. We looked closer because it was not well-lit. It was Philip and Nathaniel, and they were motioning us to come over. When they asked us to join them, we were glad for we loved to hear Nathaniel talk about his master. We guess there were thousands of people outside and we were lucky to get out without being hurt. We asked The Innkeeper to bring us some breakfast and they gave us a chance to talk. Philip said that Christ and the Pharisees were further apart on what they believed now than ever before.

Philip asks Nathanael what was the difference between what was believed. Nathaniel was eager to explain it to us. He started by saying it is easy to be a Pharisee. Now that may sound strange but it is true. The Pharisees would rather be a slave to the letter of the law than be a disciple of Christ. The question is why? The answer is they had been brought up practicing all the laws over and over all their life. It came naturally to them. They were proud of their knowledge about the way of life. For them to turn away and become a disciple of Christ would be like turning their backs on their families, their history, their heritage, and all the covenants belonging to them. For them to become a disciple of Christ means you have to put your heart into it. The law is easy to obey a few outward rules. But as a disciple of Christ, not so easy, disciples were to do the will of God and that was not natural. The law was easy because all of Israel knew it and all they had to do was to be firm. A disciple had to be humble and totally dependent on God. Christ's disciples were to love God with all their heart, soul, mind, and strength, and to love your neighbor as yourself. Nate wanted to make one more point before we broke up our meeting. The master said we were to beware of the leaven of the Pharisees which is hypocrisy. You see the Pharisees are good at telling you what to do but they did not do all they taught. Even the teachers were not keeping all the laws that they taught. So, the master was saying that it was dangerous to mix with them at all. On the other hand, the master said Whoever shall confess me before men, him shall the son of man confess before the angels of God. But he that denies me before men shall be denied before the angels of God. Friends we will one day be with Jesus and his angels in heaven as a reward for believing that Jesus is the Christ, the son of God. "Then I raised my hand and said I believe." Joseph also said, "I believe he is God's son." Nate said, "Amen to that."

Chapter 24

ANDREW, BROTHER OF PETER

HYPOCRISY OF THE PHARISEES

Luke 12:1—12

We were in Capernaum now and thousands had come to hear Jesus. He was very popular at this time. With this many people, it became dangerous to be here, for people were trampling one another. Most of all who were present were his seekers. He began by saying, beware of the leaven of the Pharisees which is hypocrisy. I thought how bold is this? There must be hundreds of the Pharisees right here today, and if there were none, they would hear about it. In fact, there were at least two who were not only Pharisees but were members of the Sanhedrin. And I saw those taking notes on everything he did.

He continued his talk by saying, everything that you have said or done will one day be known to all people. What you have spoken in the inner rooms will be proclaimed on the housetops. That made me cringe a little because I had talked loosely sometimes, not thinking what I said would ever be repeated, but we never know who was listening. I made a mental note right then and there to be careful of every word I had to say. However, I think he was talking about the Pharisees and soon people would realize they were truly guilty of what they taught and did not practice.

Jesus had so many followers that said they loved him, but would not confess that they had faith in him. They were afraid to make it public. He addressed this by saying, "And I say to you my friends do not be afraid of those who kill the body, and after that, have no more they can do. And I'll tell you whom you should fear. Fear him who after he has killed you has the power to cast you into hell. Yes, I say to you fear him." I thought at this time many people who were in this great multitude would finally step up and confess that he was the son of God. He tried to persuade them by saying, "I say to you, whoever confesses me before men, he the son of man will confess before the angels of God. He who denies me before man will be denied before the angels of God. He continued, anyone who speaks a word against the son of man will be forgiven. But to him who blasphemes against the Holy Spirit it will not be forgiven."

It was decision time and many were moving around. They could not sit still and started talking to the 12 who had been chosen as apostles. Some came to me and said that they believed he was the son of God. I assured them that they had a home in heaven, but they should be baptized and tell their friends and neighbors. He then gave us instructions on what to do, and what to say, if and when we were taken before the Sanhedrin. He said the Holy Spirit would instruct us on what to say.

What most people don't realize is what a great step this is, for they would be put out of the synagogue and lose all rights as a citizen. Since the schools were in the synagogues their children would not be permitted. They will not have any social life and no right to have a job. This would be a great hardship for believing that Jesus was God's son. If they rejected Jesus then they would have no place in heaven. Some came and believed, and some chose to stay where they were. They wanted more proof and wanted to wait a little while longer. I personally was glad that I had a job, because of all the rights they had to give up, and all the hardships that would come to families and especially those with children.

I remember when John the Baptist told me that Jesus was the Lamb of God, and I believed him. Then I ran and told Peter that we had found the Messiah. We confessed him to be the Son of God and Israel's savior, without worrying or even being afraid. Then the very next day Jesus went to Galilee and found Philip and told him to follow him. Philip was from Bethesda, just as Peter and I were. Philip had a best friend named Nathaniel and Phillip couldn't wait to tell him about the one that Moses and the prophets wrote about. Philip told him that Jesus was from Nazareth. Nathaniel's response was, "Can anything good come out of Nazareth?" And then Philip said, "Come and see." When Jesus saw Nathanael coming toward him, he said, "An Israelite indeed in whom is no deceit." Nathaniel was surprised and said, "How do you know me?" Jesus replied, "Before Philip called you when you were under the fig tree, I saw you." Nathaniel said to Jesus, "Rabbi you are the son of God. You are the king of Israel." Nathaniel believed in Jesus immediately just as Peter, Philip, and I had. We had found someone we dearly loved and wanted to serve him for the rest of our lives.

The Rich Young fool
Luke 12 13 through 21

In this gathering of 1000, a man wanted to talk to Jesus about his brother and their inheritance. Jesus was not about to get involved in domestic quarrels because the laws of inheritance were very plain. Jesus always had a story ready and this time it was about money. He said there was a rich man who owned a farm that yielded so much that his barns would not hold it all. So, he decided to pull down his barns and build bigger ones. Now he had enough room for all his crops. Then he said to his soul, "Eat, drink, and be merry." But God said, "You fool, tonight, your soul will be required of you. Then who will spend all your money?" That's the way things go when you lay up treasures for yourself and are not rich toward God. I thought how good a sermon on covetousness. This reminded me of all the farmers in Galilee who had l farms and had forgotten to give God the Glory.

The land of Galilee was supplying all of Israel with food. In fact, you could say that Galilee was the bread basket of Israel. The fish from the Sea of Galilee was sold all over Israel, along with the grain and honey. Had not God promised Israel a land flowing with milk and honey? Jesus went on to tell us not to worry about what we eat or drink or what we wear. He seemed to think there were more important things. He told us about the lilies of the field, and how beautiful God had made them to look. If he could dress grass, He could dress us up too. He said the Father knew we needed these things. He told us to seek the kingdom of God and all these things will be added to us. I think he was talking about the things people work for every day. He said it was the Father's good pleasure to give us the kingdom. He said, that where our treasure was, our hearts would be there also.

Luke 12:49-59

Jesus wanted to know if we thought he came to earth to bring peace. I thought he came here from God the Father to save the whole world. Then he made it plain that he came to bring division. He said a father would be divided against his son; a mother divided against her daughter. I can see it happening all over Israel. If we told someone that we thought he came from God the Father, then we were sure to get into an argument. In his teaching, anyone who rejected Him would experience severe judgment. He urged the whole nation to seek reconciliation with God. If they did not, they would be judged like other nations. This was a great blow to Israel for they thought they were the only nation that was right with God.

Then Jesus started to talk about the weather. "Whenever you see a cloud rising out of the west, you say a shower is coming, and so it is when you see the south wind blowing, you know that there will be hot weather." You hypocrites can discern the face of the sky and the earth, but you can't discern the times". I knew exactly what he was talking about here. He was saying he came from God and His signs had authenticated his person. He had healed the sick and raised the dead and yet Israel could not believe he was the son of God and that judgment would fall on them. After this, he told how a person was going to court to see a judge and make a decision on who was right and who was wrong. He urged all of us to make peace with our adversary before it was too late. I think what he was saying in a nutshell was that the whole nation was heading for judgment before God and should repent and believe in the son of God. I pray that everyone searches his soul to see if he is right with God. I know that I did.

Chapter 25

PETER

REPENT OR PERISH

Luke 13:1—9

Our blessed Lord had decided to go to Jerusalem and we could not stop him. All twelve of us Apostles tried to talk him out of it, but he was determined. In fact, we 12 had a meeting after he announced his plans. To make it short we decided he was going to Jerusalem to die. We had not figured out everything as we now know that he was going to die for the sins of the world. On the way there some of his enemies tried to trap him and to get him to say something bad about Pilate. So here is how the story goes.

It seems that Pilate had mingled the blood of some of the Galileans with their sacrifice in the temple at Jerusalem. Now they were waiting for Jesus to say something negative about Pilate, so as to get him into trouble. He was way too wise to fall for that trick. He asked a question. "Do you suppose that these Galileans were worse sinners than all other Galileans because they suffered such things?"

Jesus said, "No, they were not and if you don't repent you will perish." Now that was enough to get their attention. They were as guilty as the Galileans. Then he started telling us a story about a fig tree. Most all Galileans had fig trees. Fig trees were in abundance all over Galilee. Once established they would produce for many years. The same with the olive tree. Even fishermen like me had a few olive and fig trees. Galilee had tree farms for both figs and olives they made lots of money for their work. it was only natural for him to tell a story about a fig tree. The story was about a farmer who had planted a fig tree and after three years it had not produced one fig. Then the farmer told his servant to cut it down because it was worthless and only took up space. The servant begged him to give it one more year and he would dig around it and fertilize it and then if it didn't bear fruit then he would cut it down.

When we had time and we were discussing these parables Nathan thought he had the solution. He said a person was no guiltier in Galilee than in Jerusalem because he was talking about how he had been rejected in both places. God had planted Israel in this land and it was like the worthless fig tree. He had spent three years saying that he was from God, but they had rejected him. Did he have another plan for Israel? Would he give us another year with a better plan? We started to see what Nathan was talking about. He would not cut Israel off. His new plan was for the Son of God to pay for all our sins.

Spirit of Infirmity
Luke 13: 10-17

On our way to Jerusalem, Jesus stopped on the Sabbath day at the local synagogue. As he was teaching, he noticed a woman who was all bent over and could not straighten up. She had had this problem for 18 years. She reminded me of very old people who could hardly move around and I was sad for her. When Jesus noticed her, he said, "Woman you are loosed from your infirmity." Then he laid his hands on her and immediately she raised herself up straight and glorified

God. I noticed that the ruler of the synagogue did not like what he saw. He did not like it because Jesus had healed this woman on the Sabbath day. He said, "There are six days on which man ought to work. Come and be healed on them and not on the Sabbath day."

The Lord called him a hypocrite and said that everyone would lead a donkey out of the barn and water him on the Sabbath day. So, wasn't it fair to lead this daughter of Abraham who had been bound for 18 years out of her infirmity on the Sabbath day? The leader of the synagogue was put to shame, but all the multitude rejoiced for all the glorious things he had done for them.

There was a deeper meaning to the lesson and display of his power. He was actually showing Israel that he had the power to save everyone who would trust him. Israel was just like the woman with the infirmity, unable to walk upright before God. Israel had ignored the law and their walk was displeasing before God. Just as he called a woman to himself and healed her, he wanted Israel to come to him so he could heal them from all their infirmities. I thought of how easy our job would be if we didn't have religious leaders all over Israel opposing us. These people were watching us every place we went. How could they not believe after all the miracles he had performed?

The Kingdom of God
Luke 13: 18-25

Jesus told us what the kingdom of God would be like in the future. He compared it to a mustard seed a man planted in his garden that grew into a tree and the birds came to nest in it. This parable was really saying that his followers would see a great increase in a short time. It seems like the world will come and join his group, but they will not really be believers.

Then he said that God's Kingdom was like leaven which a woman took and hid in three measures of meal and soon all the meal was leavened. I think his meaning was evil would creep in slowly through unsaved people and make the group grow, but not in a good way.

It seems that leaven would slowly penetrate the meal and cause it to grow very large because bad doctrine would be introduced and after a time would come to be accepted.

Most of our followers seem concerned about all the people who heard his message and then rejected it. The number who accepted his message was small in comparison. So, they asked Jesus a question about the very few who had committed themselves to him. So, the question was," Lord are there just a few being saved?" He did not answer the question but told us to strive to enter the narrow gate. The gate to enter God's kingdom was none other than our Lord Jesus Christ. That means they will not get in by keeping the Law of Moses, and it sounds like it would be difficult, but no one will be turned away. He went on to say that one day the offer would be withdrawn. He likened it to a homeowner who locked the doors for the night and all who had not entered would be left out forever. Really, he was saying the time will come when no more will be saved, and all who hear will be wise to enter the narrow gate when they hear the message. Yes, there will be more who rejected the invitation than received it. All who later want to come in will be turned away forever to burn in the fires of hell. From the outside, the non-believer will get to see all the saved and want to be in that number which includes Abraham, Isaac, and Jacob plus the prophets and lots and lots of Gentiles from all over the nations. Jesus had a broken heart for he lamented over Jerusalem who killed the prophets and stoned the others. He wanted to take them and love them like a mother hen would gather her chicks under their wings but they would not let him. He said their house would be left desolate, and empty, and they would not see him again until the time when he came back to earth as Messiah of all.

Luke 13:31-35

Some Pharisees came and told him that he should leave for King Herod wanted to kill him. Jesus knew all about Herod and his cunning ways. He also knew Herod could not touch him because it was not the will of God. Not all Pharisees were out to get Jesus. Actually, many trusted him as a Savior. Two of them were Joseph and Nicodemus. All Jews will be happy to see Jesus when he comes to set up his Kingdom on earth. They will say, "Blessed is he who comes in the name of the Lord."

Chapter 26

THADDAEUS

STORIES OF LOST THINGS

Luke 15:1-32

First of all, I want to be clear about my name. My given name is Judas, and my other names are Thaddaeus and Lebbaeus. Most of my friends call me Thad. I like that one best because that is what my friends called me when I was a child.

The story I would like to tell you about happened while we were traveling to Jerusalem. As we came near to Jerusalem the crowds were bigger and bigger. And the pressure from the Sanhedrin was greater and greater. They were watching his every move, and it seemed they were against everything he did. It was true that he was welcoming sinners and tax collectors. He even ate with them when invited then he told us a story about a lost sheep.

Luke 15: 3–7

A man had 100 sheep and lost one, and then he left the 99 in the wilderness and went to look for it. When he found it, he laid it on his shoulders rejoicing. When he got home, he called all his friends and neighbors and said for them to rejoice with him for he had found his lost sheep. He said there would be more joy in heaven over one sinner who repented over the 99 righteous persons who need no repentance.

The Sanhedrin's attitude toward sinners and tax collectors was that God was pleased when one of them perished. They taught that God hated sinners and withdrew himself from them. Since Jesus invited sinners and welcomed them, and even ate with them, they thought he could not be of God. The question for them was, would they leave the flock and go after the lost sheep until they found it, or let it perish? Jesus taught us to go find the sheep and lovingly carry it home. He had so much joy in finding the sheep that he did not scold it, or punish it. Then there was true joy in heaven. Jesus showed the true heart of God for sinners. God loves sinners but hates their sins. God wants to restore all sinners.

The Lost Coin
Luke 15:8-10

He gave us another short story about a woman who had ten pieces of silver and lost one of them. First, she gets a lamp and looks for it. Then she sweeps the floor and finally finds it. Then she is so happy that she calls all her friends and neighbors and tells them to rejoice with her for she has found the piece of money. Then he finished the story by saying, "I say unto you, there is more joy in the presence of angels of God over one sinner that repents." What he means is that God loves it when a sinner repents. In fact, all heaven rejoices.

The Lost Son
Luke 15: 11-32

He told us about this heartwarming story about a father-son relationship. This certain man had two sons. The younger one wanted his inheritance now, and his father divided the inheritance between the two sons. The younger of the two took his money and went to a far country, where he wasted it on riotous living. After he had spent it all, there was a famine in that land and he found himself broke and hungry. Then he got himself a job feeding swine. He was so hungry that he wanted to eat their food but was prevented from doing so.

Then he came to himself and decided to go back to his father's house and ask for a job, as a servant to his father. He was prepared to tell his father that he was not worthy to be called his son, so make me one of your hired servants. Then he headed for home. Meanwhile, his father saw him coming in the distance and ran out to meet him. He loved his son and put his arms around him and kissed him. He told his father he had sinned against heaven and in your sight and was no longer worthy to be called your son. But his father instructed his servants to bring him the best robe, bring him a ring, and put some shoes on his feet. Then he told them to kill the fatted calf and let us be merry. For his son was dead and is now alive again. He was lost and now he is found, and they began to be merry.

Now his elder son was out in the field and as he drew near the house, he heard music and dancing. He asked what was going on. The servants replied that your brother has come home. Your father has killed the fatted calf because he is safe at home. The eldest son was angry and would not go into the house. His father came to him and said, "Your brother is home." And his son said, "These many years I have served you and you did not even give me a kid so I could make merry with my friends. But as soon as this son comes home after wasting his money on harlots, you have killed the fatted calf." His father told him that he had always been with him, and all I have is yours. And it is the right thing to do. We should make merry and be glad for your brother was dead and is alive and was lost and is now found.

I think this a wonderful story about the heart of God. It seems like God is saying no matter what you do or say I will forgive you if you repent and ask for forgiveness. This repentance is from the heart and is shown by turning from your sins and coming home to your heavenly father. He is always ready with outstretched arms, always looking for his lost sheep.

Chapter 27

JOHN, BROTHER OF JAMES
CONCERNING MONEY

Luke 16:1—31

We were still on our way to Jerusalem and Jesus was in no hurry to get there. He was still preaching the kingdom message to all who would hear. We were getting good responses from lots of people, both Jews and Gentiles. Some said he was like a breath of fresh air, and they learned so much. They were happy to hear the message but did not commit to believing in him.

That day he wanted to tell everyone about riches. He himself had never handled any money as far as I know. Some people had tried to give him money but he would tell them to give it to Judas who was in charge of the purse. Judas was well-trained in handling money because his father was a businessman. and he had also trained his son very well. I thought we could have selected a better person for that job, but I was not in charge. I will admit that he was good at taking some expensive things that were given to us and trading them for other things that were easier to carry or sell. He always got a good price. You may have heard, "You can't get blood out of a turnip." I will say that Judas always came away with more money than I thought the goods were worth. He definitely was a better money manager than I was. Brother James could vouch for that.

Jesus continued his talk about money. He was to expose some of the Pharisees' business practices which Moses taught. They taught that if one was rich, he was in God's favor because riches were a sign that they were pleasing God. If you read Deuteronomy, you will see where they got the notion because it clearly says that God would bless Israel in almost everything that they do if, "We keep all His commandments." (Deuteronomy 28: 1-14). He started by telling of an unjust steward who was about to lose his job. So, he went to all the people who owed his employer and reduced the amount they owed. Then after he was dismissed from his job, he had friends to show him favors. Jesus was in no way saying a person should be a dishonest person. He was showing how a person handling money would be rewarded later. The lesson was doing right and good to the people around you and it would be like laying up treasures in heaven. He always taught that people should be honest in all dealings. He said that if a person cannot be trusted in small things, then he cannot be trusted in any amount. Then he said a person cannot serve two masters. You will love one and hate the other. He was saying that a person cannot serve God and money. Money has a way of separating people from God. The more money you have the less you depend on God. I think that is why Jesus had Judas handling the money so as to not be thinking about money.

The Pharisees were lovers of money and just had to comment on his talk. So, they derided Him. He answered by saying, "You are those who justify yourselves before men, but God knows your heart. For what is highly esteemed by men is an abomination in the sight of God. The Law and the Prophets were until John. Since then, the kingdom of God has been preached and everyone is pressing into it. It is easier for heaven and earth to pass away than for one tittle of the law to fail. Whoever divorces his wife and marries commits adultery. And whoever marries her who is divorced from her husband commits adultery." They were offended when he said the law and the prophets were until John. Since that time the kingdom of God was being preached and everyone was pressing into it. They thought that all Jews were already in God's kingdom because they were the seed of Abraham. I think he already knew some of them had divorced their wives and married new ones and so broke the law. Then he tells them a story that would show that being a son of Abraham would mean being a person of faith. Further meaning that faith that Jesus is God's Son.

A Rich Man and a Poor Man
Luke 16:19-31

There was a rich man and a poor man. They both died. The poor beggar went to paradise or as the Jews like to say Abraham's bosom. The rich man went to Hades. Hades is what is commonly called hell. The two people did not go to these two places just because they were rich and poor. The rich man went to Hades because he did not trust God. I suppose he was not looking for our Savior to come and pay for our sins. Therefore, he was not practicing the law. Did you notice how the rich man treated the poor man? The dogs treated the beggar better in that they licked his wounds. The poor man was most likely a praying man looking daily for his Savior to come and help him. I know for a fact that God is a good and fair judge. The story continues that the rich man in Hades looked afar off and saw the poor beggar in paradise. He cried out to Abraham calling him father. He asked to have Lazarus dip the tip of his finger in the water and come and cool his tongue for he was in torment in the flames. Why did he call Abraham his father? Because Abraham was the first Jew. He was known as the father of the Jews. The rich man must have been a Jew because he called Abraham his father. The rich man was of the mind that God must love him because he had made him rich. He did not know that Abraham was also the father of faith. Abraham believed in God and he believed in what God said.

When he realized that he wasn't getting any help for himself he asked Abraham to send Lazarus to his father's house because he had five brothers that he wanted to warn. He did not want them to come to the place of torment. Abraham told them they had Moses and the prophets and they could hear them. Moses and the prophets had taught generosity and care for the poor and disabled. But he said, "Father Abraham if one will go to them from the dead they will repent." Abraham said to them, "If they will not hear Moses and the prophets neither will they be persuaded though one rise from the dead." I thought this would be a good time to pray for them that their eyes would be opened. Praying that believing in Jesus was the new and only way to get into God's Kingdom.

Chapter 28

JOHN, BROTHER OF JAMES
HOW TO GET ALONG

Luke 17:1—10

Soon after the story about the rich man and Lazarus, the beggar, Jesus must have heard us bickering about some of the jobs we had to do. Sometimes we would have a really good argument. Then he wanted to talk about how we offend one another. He started by getting all 12 of us together. That was a hard job in itself for we were around the Sea of Galilee and some of us were visiting our families from time to time with his blessings. Jealousy would creep in and a few offensive words would sneak out. He said, "It is impossible that no offenses should come but woe to him through whom they do come. It would be better for him if a millstone was hung around his neck and he was thrown into the sea than he should offend one of these little ones."

After he was through, I asked him if he was talking about our squabbles or if there was something else. His answer was both. We needed to do our jobs without bickering. However, he said that he had been pointing out what the Pharisees had been doing that wasn't what his father had intended for them to do. Some had heard and joined our group by believing he was God's son and were willing to change their lifestyle. Then he said, "Concerning these little ones I was talking about those who were willing to leave the Pharisees teaching and follow me. They are easily offended and we need a lot of patience when dealing with them." Then he went on to say that we should take heed to ourselves and if your brother sins against you rebuke him. And if he repents forgive him. And if he sins against you seven times in a day, and seven times in a day returns to you saying I repent you shall forgive him. So, my brother, James said, "Lord increases our faith." We thought our faith had to be increased if we were to do the nearly impossible. The task of forgiving up to seven times in one day was completely different from what they taught in the law of offense and forgiveness. It turned out that it was not about the amount of our faith but in whom our faith was placed. We had mustard seed faith, but that faith will grow with usage. Is he a genius? No, he is God in the flesh; I have come to see his ways are not our ways. Then he talked about the duties of his servant and how a servant went into the field and plowed all day and came home. He would not sit down to eat. He would first prepare supper for his master and attend to him while he ate. Then he would eat himself. Then he asked, if the master would thank the servant for all of this? He said, "I think not." The servant had only done his duty. We were to do the same. I thought most likely we will be better men for a while instead of squabbling boys.

Luke 17:9–11

Jesus was trying to keep out of Galilee because Herod wanted to kill him. He wanted to stay out of Judea because the Sanhedrin was plotting to kill him. He was stopping at all the small towns and villages along the way. He was staying mostly in Samara and Galilee and giving us time to visit our families. One day he met ten men who were lepers. They ask for him to come and cure them. They did not come near him at all. He commanded them to go and show themselves to the priest. He was testing their faith. They all started off to do as he said. Then they started to be healed and new life came back into it them. One is them was a Samaritan and he returned to Jesus and fell at his feet and thanked him. Then Jesus said, "Weren't there ten, and where are the nine?" It was tough to see nine Israelites that were not thankful but one Samaritan who was. He was having better success in Samaria than in Israel. What makes our people so stiff necked?

Luke 17: 20-37

At one place we had a gathering of many people and the Pharisees wanted to know when the kingdom of God would come. And he answered that the kingdom of God is not coming with a visible display. And so, people will say, "Look here it is, nor there it is, you see the kingdom of God is now among you." What he was saying was he was king and he was here among the people of Israel and they did not recognize Him. In fact, they had rejected the King. So now the kingdom of God would not come with observation or outward show but would be there in the hearts of men. Then he told us very plainly how the kingdom of God would appear. He said it would be as plain as lightning flashing out of one part of heaven and shining to the other part under heaven. Also, the Son of Man will be in his day. Before that time he must suffer many things. He had told us previously that he would suffer many things and be put to death, but would rise from the dead in three days.

Meanwhile, the people as a whole will be eating and drinking and marrying and giving in marriage just like it was in the days of Noah. He also mentioned Lot and Sodom and how they acted just like the people in the days of Noah. They ate and drank bought and sold and planted and built. As soon as Lot left it rained fire and brimstone from heaven and destroyed them. It will be the same old story when the son of man is revealed. If you are on the housetop don't go back for your personal goods. Just remember what happened to Lot's wife. Don't try to save your life or you will lose it. There will be two men in bed and one will be taken and the other will be left. Two women will be grinding grain and one will be taken and the other left. I think the ungodly will be taken and the ones left will go into God's kingdom. He also said, "Wherever the body is, there the eagles will be gathered together."

We, disciples, discussed what that meant. Most of us thought it was the judgment of the unbelievers. As far as those who are taken and those who are left behind, He was aware that it would be night on half of the earth and it would be daytime on the other half, and some will be sleeping and some will be waking. All this made good sense to us. I have prayed about the gathering of eagles and it seems that there will be a large war just before he comes again with lots of bodies lying around that will be eaten by eagles and other flesh-eating birds.

Chapter 29

NATHANAEL

LESSONS ON PRAYER

Luke 18:1–8

Did you ever get frustrated with prayer? I think all of us at some time in our prayer life have been disgusted with prayer. Some folks actually get angry with God. I personally have not come to that point in my own life. I would ask for something to happen in my own family and then pray for it again and again. Then threw up my hands in disgust because these prayers were not answered. One day Jesus decided to tell us a story about prayer. We were all happy to hear just how to do this.

He started out by saying, "In a certain city there was a judge who did not fear God nor regard man." There was a widow in that same city who had been wronged and came to see the judge to get justice. But she received no justice for a while. The woman would not give up but kept coming back. After a while, the judge gave her what she asked for because of her persistence. She had worn him down until he was exasperated with her persistence. Then Jesus asked a question, "Shall not God avenge his own elect who cry out to him day and night though he bears along with them." His lesson seems to say, don't give up. God is listening. God is our loving heavenly father and we are his children. He will give us what is good for us.

Luke 18:8–14

Then he gave us an example of how not to pray. His story was about a Pharisee and a tax collector. They both went into the temple to pray. The Pharisees mostly told God what a great person he was. Then he said he was not an extortioner. He was not unjust or an adulterer or even a tax collector. He said he fasts twice a week and tithes his money. He sure was a good man in his own eyes. He talked like God was lucky to have him as a believer. He sure impressed me with all he was doing. He did not confess even one sin. I think this Pharisee would win hands down if there was a contest as to who was the best man.

Now let's hear what the tax collector had to say. The tax collector stood afar off and would not so much as raise his eyes to heaven. He beat on his chest and said, "God be merciful to me a sinner." Jesus said, "This man went down to his house Justified. The other did not. For everyone who exalts himself will be humbled and he who humbles himself will be exalted.

I truly believe God likes it when we stay out of trouble. I think we should be generous to God with our money and goods. It is good when we fast for it helps me to keep my mind on God. However, we should not look down on others. Sometimes confession of sin is the biggest part of my prayers. Sin is always near us. Sin is easy for almost everyone around us is sinning. Sometimes it is difficult to live for God. That is why prayer is so important to all of us. Let's try to do it more often as we wait for the kingdom of God when Jesus will be king.

Luke 18: 15–17

Jesus gave us another example of little children. The children were coming to Jesus. Some hugged him, some shook his hand, and still others were shy and just kind of walked up to him with that shy look not knowing what to do. The parents also brought babies to him that were not old enough to walk. We disciples and apostles were protective of him not wanting him to waste this time with children. We tried to dissuade them by shielding him from coming near. Jesus was angry with us for trying to keep the little children from him.

He said, "Let the little children come to me and do not forbid them for of such is the kingdom of God. Assuredly I say to you whoever does not receive the kingdom of God as a little child will by no means enter it."

I have noticed there is no one who has more faith than little children. They don't come bragging or doubting. They come with faith. They believed in Jesus. They were truly children of Abraham who believed in God and was the father of faith.

Luke 18: 18–23

After Jesus blessed all the children and a whole lot of proud parents. I would like to add that some of those children were sick, some deformed and not one left him in the same condition as when he came. Then a young man came to him and wanted to know how he could inherit eternal life. I suppose that all people have thought about that at one time or another. He said something I didn't catch right off." He said the good teacher." Jesus caught it for he said, "Why do you call me good? No one is good but one, that is God." I think Jesus recognized him as being a member of the Sanhedrin because he was a ruler. Eternal life is the same as how can I get into your kingdom. This man knew Jesus was offering a kingdom that was everlasting and Jesus would be a king. He also knew this was a righteous kingdom and one had to be righteous to get in. Jesus told the man that he knew the scriptures and he quoted some of them to the man. The young man said he had kept these from his youth. Jesus said he lacked one thing. "Sell all you have and distribute it to the poor and you will have treasures in heaven, then come and follow me." When the young man heard this, he was very sorrowful for he was very rich.

The man loved his riches better than he loved the poor. He did not love his neighbor as himself. He was not righteous enough to enter God's Kingdom. His own righteousness would never work. Jesus became very sorrowful as the young man walked away. He said," How hard it is for those who have riches to enter the kingdom of God for it is easier for a camel to go through the eye of a needle than for a rich man to enter the kingdom of God."

This was very hard for us 12 to swallow. We immediately wondered if we had too much to enter God's Kingdom. Someone in our group said, "Who then can be saved." Jesus explained that believing in riches to get into heaven was impossible. God had made it possible to get into heaven. Salvation was God's work. It happens when man responds to faith in Christ. No work is needed. No money is needed. Only faith in Jesus Christ was all that was needed. I think Peter was thinking hard about this for he said, "See we have left all to follow you. "We had money when we were fishing. We had servants from time to time. Even now our servants are fishing and giving money to our cause." Then Jesus assured us that we shall receive many times more in the present age, and in the age to come eternal life.

Luke 18:31–34
Jesus Predicts His Death, Burial, and Resurrection

Then he called a meeting for just the 12. He said, "We are going up to Jerusalem and all the things that are written by the prophets concerning the son of man will be accomplished. For he will be delivered to the Gentiles and will be mocked and insulted and spit upon. They will scourge him and kill him. And on the third day, he will rise again."

None of us could remember what he said. It was after the crucifixion that it all came back to us. I think each one of us can now say it word for word. He also had another incident happen to him as we came into Jericho. A blind man who was a beggar heard all of us as we were going by. He asked what it meant. Jericho was a town that was crowded this time of the year because when the weather cooled down a lot of the wealthy people came down to Jericho. Jericho had very warm temperatures.

It was fortunate that this man had good hearing. He knew something was happening. He was told that Jesus of Nazareth was passing by. That was like music to his ear for he had heard that Jesus had given sight to many. Therefore, he said," Jesus Son of David have mercy on me." Some of the people tried to quiet him but he cried even louder." Son of David have mercy on me." Jesus stopped and they brought the blind man to him. Jesus asked what he wanted he said that he wanted to receive his sight. Jesus said," Receive your sight for your faith has made you well." He had faith in Jesus and that Faith had made him well, all he wanted to do then was follow Jesus and glorify him. The whole story was a good lesson for Israel as a nation and also a lesson for Jews and Gentiles individually. They were both blind spiritually and they could care less. When we tried to tell them they would say, I'm okay. I'm a child of Abraham. Others would say that they went to synagogue every week and to the temple for all the feast days. They could not see their need and so Christ could not help them. Jericho was of the tribe of Levi. There were more priests in this town than anywhere else. Yet it was teeming with publicans also. Jericho was also a great trade city something like Capernaum. Farmers from across the Jordan River sold a lot of fruits, vegetables, and grain and the Roman government wanted their share of the revenue. The man who was chief tax collector was a man named Zacchaeus. Dr. Luke has told me that Zacchaeus wants to tell his own story. Read carefully because he has a wonderful story to tell.

Chapter 30

ZACCHAEUS

CLIMBING A TREE

Luke 19:1—10

It was a beautiful morning in Jericho with not a cloud in the sky. You must know that bodily I felt great yet there was something bothering me. I suppose you could say that I was troubled in the soul. My family life was just super. My wife Judy and I were on the friendliest of terms. Even Jamie and Joshua the two grandsons God had given me were on their best behavior lately. It seemed that my body was well rested but my soul was very restless. How does a person rest his soul? I felt this question was too big for me. My business was collecting taxes for the Roman government. Maybe that is my problem and the reason I felt this way. Yet there was no pressure on me because I was the chief tax collector. The general who was my boss resided in Rome and was very pleased with the job I was doing. I was pleased with the way my men were handling the taxes in Jericho. So, there must be something I can do or someone I can see to help me with this problem. Just then a young man came running through the streets of Jericho shouting excitedly that Jesus of Nazareth was coming through our city. Then I became excited. I had been busy the last time he came. through. He was going beyond Jordan to minister to those people. I had heard the story of how he had dealt with a man they call, Legion, who lived among the tombs. Legion had been freed from a lot of demons and now he was in his right mind and a model citizen. His whole life has been changed. All he wanted to do was tell others about Jesus. He was totally sure that Jesus was Israel's promised Messiah. Then there was the time he came from Perea and passed through Jericho and I ran out to see him but there were so many people in front of me that I could not see him because I was too short. I was determined that this would not happen again. Now where was a good place to see him? Perhaps a hill? The streets were full of people. There were people without a number following him. The rumor was that he was going to Jerusalem to set up his kingdom. Most of the people were waiting to see if he would heal anyone. All those sick people were being helped out to the road, as the crowds swelled, I had a sinking feeling that I would never get one glimpse of him unless I took some drastic action.

There was a voice beside me who said," Who is it," I looked down and saw a blind man and told him it was Jesus. He started crying out for Jesus to have mercy on him but those in front of Jesus sternly told him to be quiet. But he kept crying out for the son of David to have mercy on him. I thought if he came over, I would get to see him also. But Jesus stopped and asked that the blind man be brought to him. I knew if I wanted to see him, I would have to do something differently. Just then I saw that sycamore tree with its branches hanging out over the road. Would it be childish to climb a tree just to see Jesus? I had heard him say we must come to him just as a child if we want to get into God's Kingdom. I was a dignified man. I was chief of all the tax collectors. My desire to see him was greater than my fear of losing my dignity. Perhaps if I could get on that branch that hangs out over the road, I could see him really well without him seeing me. After all, there was a lot of cover there. reluctantly I started to climb a tree. I had not climbed a tree since I was a boy and I soon learned that I was not a boy anymore. It wasn't as much fun as I remembered. In just a minute or two I was where I wanted to be. I was snuggled in behind some big leaves and no one would see me. It seemed like hours sitting there but perhaps it was more like a few minutes because all the time I was arguing with myself about whether I was doing the right thing. It was too late to get down now so I guess I would just stay in the tree and see Jesus.

It didn't take long to figure out which one was Jesus because he was the one answering all the questions. I wondered if he could help me with my problem of a tired soul. Just as he was going under the tree, I was feeling very safe and relieved that no one had spotted me. He looked up and said," Zacchaeus make haste and come down for today I must stay at your house." All those people were staring up at me and I felt very uncomfortable. Naturally, I hurried down from that tree and was soon on his side. As we made our way through the streets of Jericho he would stop from time to time and heal one who was sick. He would speak a word of encouragement to someone and the next person would have his question answered. The blind man who had received his sight was following close behind Jesus and saying," Glory to God, God glory to God. "It seemed the whole city was on the streets wanting to see this God-man.

Soon we were at my house and we entered and Judy and my grandsons met him. The crowd stayed out in the street but 12 of his apostles came inside. Since they were going to stay the night, there were meals to prepare and sleeping quarters to get ready. We would be crowded but we would manage. My two grandsons were with him constantly. They were asking so many questions that I had to tell them to leave him alone, but he insisted that he loved children and welcomed their questions. At mealtime, he said a short prayer to God for our food. It was bedtime when we had a little time to talk. I still had a lot of unanswered questions although I learned a lot from just listening to Jamie and Josh talk to him. Just knowing that I was with the Son of God made me want to open up my life to him. I felt I was guilty of many sins and confessed to him. I told him I would give half my goods to the poor; I would also pay back four-fold the ones I had falsely taken money from. Jesus said to me," Today salvation has come to this house, because he also is a son of Abraham, for the son of man has come to seek and to save that which was lost."

He asked me if I had heard of his invitation. I had not, so he said that he usually gave this invitation." Come to me all who are weary and heavy laden and I will give you rest. Take my yoke upon you and learn from me for I am gentle and humble in heart and you shall find rest for your souls. For my yoke is easy and my burden is light." That is exactly what I needed. My burden lifted and rest for my soul and I could have it by taking his yoke upon me. To be yoked with the Son of God was the most exciting and meaningful thing I had ever heard and gladly accepted his offer. The joy I felt was unexplainable. I had never felt so good, so relieved, my burdens were lifted and I knew I was right with God. I could now walk with Jesus every day. The blind man would say" Glory to God." Oh yes, the next time someone tells you to go climb a tree, do it for it may be the beginning of something really exciting and wonderful for your life.

Chapter 31

NATHANAEL

THE KING IS COMING

Luke 19:11—28

Dr. Luke since you asked me to write a story about what happened after we left Jericho, here is what I remember.

We talked that morning about the climb. The climb as it was known was from Jericho to Jerusalem. First, this road had many names. It was called a rocky road, dangerous road, Robbers Road, haunted road, and a few others. It was even called, the way of blood. It was about six hours up to Jerusalem. And when I say up it means up. We were to go from 800 ft below sea level to about 2500 ft above sea level. We dreaded leaving a warm climate for a cooler place. Also, we were leaving the comfort of Zacchaeus and the good food his wife and servants gave us. The whole city had trees blooming and the aroma seemed to say, "Stay a while longer."

We twelve thought Jesus was going to receive a crown and be king when we got to Jerusalem. We had heard so many sermons about the Kingdom of God that we thought it was going to happen, maybe today. It was introduced by John the Baptist, Jesus' forerunner and Jesus had been preaching it for nearly three years. He must have heard what we were talking about and told us another parable before we got to Jerusalem.

He said a certain nobleman went into a far country to receive for himself a kingdom and return. So, he called ten of his servants and delivered to them ten minas and said to them, "Do business until I come".

The nobleman was none other than Jesus. His 10 servants were 10 disciples or apostles, or just 10 followers. The business they were to do was to make money with what he gave each of them. The money was about three months of wages.

The people hated him and said that they would not have this man ruling over them. Then he went on his way. After a period of time, he received his kingdom and came back to see how his servants had done with his money. The one he gave 10 miners had gained 10 more, so he gave him authority over 10 cities. If they had gained five, He gave them authority over five cities. But yet another came and said, "Here is your mina, I have kept for you in a handkerchief. I feared you because you are a hard man. You collect where you did not deposit, and reap where you did not sow, I say to you that everyone who has will be given more and from him who doesn't have even what he has will be taken away. Bring the enemies of mine who did not want me to reign over them and slay them before me."

Since Jesus was telling the story about himself, we summarize that he was going away before he set up his kingdom. We wondered for how long, and we also reasoned that we were his servants that he was counting on to be faithful stewards of what he had given us. Namely his message. I also wondered if I would be ruler over many cities. As far as his enemies we had to say it was the citizens of Israel who had rejected him as Son of God. They would stand before him for judgment.

And it came to pass when he came near to Bethpage and Bethany at the mount called Mount of Olives, he sent Peter and John to

Bethpage to find an unbroken colt and to bring it back to him. He also said if anyone asks you what you're doing tell them the Lord has need of it. As soon as they unloosed the colt someone asked what was the meaning of it. They told him the Lord has need of him, and they let them go and they returned and told us that there were people all over the land who had come for the Passover. They had tents and temporary shelters all around Jerusalem. Most of the Mount of Olives was covered. Even here in Bethany, people had found shelter but it was not as crowded as Jerusalem. When we brought the colt which had never been broken he never acted afraid or untrained. He just allowed Jesus to feel at ease on his back. We, disciples, talked this over and came up with an answer that we were happy with. He had never addressed himself as Lord and doing so now he claimed to be Israel's Messiah. As far as the unbroken colt he showed he had all authority over all creation. Jesus rode the colt and all the rest of us walked. The crowds began going with us and some spread their cloaks on the road as a sign of respect. Until this time Jesus had not sought to be called Messiah but now, he allowed it. By riding on the colt Jesus was fulfilling the prophecy of Zechariah 9:9-10 that predicted that the Messiah would be riding on a donkey. The crowd was praising God for all the miracles and signs they had seen.

The Pharisees understood the meaning of what was going on and asked that Jesus stop people from calling him Messiah or King. Jesus said, "I tell you if these should keep silent these stones would immediately cry out. "We were still on Mount Olive when Jerusalem came into view. Jesus looked at the city and began to weep. Saying," If you had known even you, especially in this your day the things that make for peace but now they are hidden from your eyes. For the day will come up on you when your enemies will build an embankment around you, surround you on every side, and level you and your children within you, to the ground. And they will not leave in you one stone upon another, because you did not know the time of your visitation."

Luke 19:45-48

When we finally came to the temple it was very difficult, because so many people were in the streets that it was hard to move. Our group was also noisy because we were shouting, "Hosanna blessed is he who comes in the name of the Lord. Blessed is the kingdom of our father David that comes in the name of our Lord, Hosanna in the highest."

By this time the Pharisees were really upset with us and we were not too pleased with them. Jesus Christ presented himself as Messiah at his baptism openly. He had also authenticated himself at his temptation for 40 days. His glory was revealed in his Transfiguration. His triumphal entry was an official presentation as Messiah. These people should have known who presented himself. They thought he was a prophet from Nazareth. Lots of people came to Christ in the temple to be healed but the Pharisees and the teachers of all the law were opposed to him and hurried to complete their plans to put him to death. He went to where they were selling doves and overturned the money changers' tables. He drove out those who were buying and selling. He said to them, "It is written my house is a house of prayer, but you have made it a den of Thieves "He would not even let them carry merchandise through the temple. He demonstrated His authority to possess and safeguard his father's house. The religious authorities objected to what he was doing but the people approved it. In our discussion, this was an easy one to figure out. The money that was used to buy sacrificial animals had to be a certain coinage. Gentiles could not buy one of these animals without that coin. The money changers had this money ready for anyone who needed it. But they charge a high price for it. They had to exchange the money that would buy the animal. Then they would purchase the animal that would be sacrificed for their sins.

This business was set up in the court of the Gentiles who came to pray. There wasn't given any privacy or respect. The Lord did not just walk away after he cleaned the temple of business but stayed there so they could not start it back up. This week being a Passover week how many thousands of animals were to be sold? This made him very unpopular with the religious leaders, especially when he called them a den of robbers. He not only ran the business people out but he started teaching the people who were delighted to hear him.

Luke 20:1–8

We all stayed in our tents on the Mount of Olives because Jesus wanted to get started early in the temple. When we arrived the chief priests, Scribes, and the elders were all there to try to prevent him from teaching. That meant we had Pharisees, Sadducees, and Herodians all ready for him. Before he could begin, they wanted to know by whose authority he was doing these things. Consent to preach in the temple required previous authority. All teaching must be authoritative. Approved authority was handed down from generation to generation. From teacher to disciple. But he answered and said to them," I will ask you one thing, and answer me. The baptism of John, was it from heaven or men?" And they reasoned among themselves saying, if we say from heaven, he will say why then did you not believe him? But if we say from men, all the people will stone us, for they are persuaded that John was a prophet. They said, "They did not know from where." And Jesus said neither will I tell you by what authority I do these things. By their answers, they showed that they were insincere wanting only to trap him or stop him anyway. Jesus always took care to answer for sincere seekers but had no time for cynical critics or those trying to manipulate.

Chapter 32

NATHANAEL AND MARY MAGDALENE
THE WICKED VINE DRESSER

Luke 20:9—27

When Jesus was through telling about his authority to teach in the temple, he told all of us about a man who planted a Vineyard and leased it to a vinedresser. Then he went away for a long time. When it was time for harvest, he sent a servant to get some grapes or wine, but the vine dresser beat him and sent him away empty-handed. Then the owner sent him another servant and they beat him treated him shamefully, and sent him away empty-handed. Then he sent a third servant and they wounded him and cast him out. The owner said to himself, what shall I do? I will send my beloved son probably they will respect him when they see him.

But when the tenants who leased the vineyards saw him, he thought. This is the heir, come let us kill him he said to his cohorts, and that the vineyard may be ours. Then they cast him out of the vineyard and killed him. Now what will the owner of the vineyard do to them? He will come and destroy the vinedressers and give the vineyard to others. When they heard it, they said," Certainly not," then he looked at them and said, "What then, is this that which was written? The stone that the builders rejected has become the Chief Cornerstone. Whoever falls on that stone will be broken? But on whomever it falls it will grind him to powder." And when they heard it, they said, "God forbid."

Then the chief priest and scribes that very hour sought to lay hands on him. But they feared the people for they knew he had spoken this Parable against them. Jesus spoke this parable mostly for the Sanhedrin, and we had some members here, in our midst. We had chief priests and teachers of the law, called scribes both Pharisees and Sadducees, and the elders, Laymen, and political leaders. It looked like all of Israel was here for the Passover. This Vineyard was certainly Israel. The Israelites all knew it for it had been used before to describe them. The owner of the vineyard was God. The servant he sent was his prophet. The son he sent was Jesus. They will kill the son of God. They did not *want Him* to rule over them. They thought they would be free to do as they please.

God or Caesar
Luke 20:20–26

After they were embarrassed and angry, He said, "The stone which the builders rejected has become the chief cornerstone." Jesus was telling them that they could kill him but, they could not kill the purpose of God. They had rejected Jesus who was the chief cornerstone. It was decision time again. They could humbly submit to Him and be saved or reject Him and let the stone fall on them and they would be ground to powder. I think I would rather be saved by Him than be ground to powder.

Then they watched him and even sent spies who pretended to be righteous that they might seize on his words in order to deliver him to the power and the authority of the governor. Some think these people were spies, and not the Pharisees he knew, but were friends of those he knew. They really wanted to know his thinking so perhaps the Herodian really did want a straight answer. However, their questions were not pure because they came from the old Pharisees. I think Jesus saw through it when he heard the question.

They said, "We know that you do not show personal favoritism, but teach the way of God in the truth. "Is it lawful to pay taxes to Caesar or not?" He perceived their craftiness and asked, why do you test me? In Israel, there was a great controversy over this question. Some said. "No, we have only one king, and that is Jehovah," but if he said that he would be in trouble with Rome. If he said, "Yes," to Rome then the Jews would be against him and some would say he disowned Jehovah, Israel's true king.

If he denied Rome the right to collect taxes, he'd be chargeable to Rome and would have been guilty of inciting a rebellion. He said, show me a Denarius. Whose image and inscription does it have? They all had one answer, "Caesar" And he said to them, "Render therefore to Caesar the things that are Caesar's and to God the things that are God's." They could not catch him in his words in the presence of the people, and they marveled at his answer and kept silent as he knew they would.

In this world, there are two types of authority. Believers have two citizenships, one on earth and one in heaven. We are bound to keep God's laws and we are to keep man's law. God has ordained man to set up a government. All countries have a system in place to help the citizens build peaceful and productive lives. Some of the Jews thought they were already citizens of heaven and therefore not under man's laws. We have our citizenship here on earth now, so we are to obey the laws of the country we are living in. Therefore, we are to pay taxes to that country. We are to obey the authorities such as policemen, governors, presidents, and all others that are authorities. Then we are also bound to keep the laws of God. The Ten Commandments are there for all who fear God and seek to know him and obey him. We also need to recognize Jesus as his son and remember that one day he will rule and reign over us as our king. Our rewards in his kingdom will be based on what we do here on earth during our lifetime. I think one of his greatest commands was to love one another as he has loved us. That raises the bar a little higher, meaning that the Ten Commandments said we were to love our neighbors as ourselves, but Jesus told his disciples to love one another as He loved them. you should love your neighbor and yourself. But you are to love your brothers and sisters in Christ as much as Christ loves us. Please think and pray about this.

Luke 20: 27-40

If you know anything about the Sadducees, you already know their doctrine on the resurrection. They did not believe in it. Why did they bring up a subject that they did not believe in? They were trying to concoct a ridiculous story to make Jesus look ridiculous. The story was about a man who married a woman and died before he had any children. In Israel, the Law says that a man who dies without children will then have his brother marry his widow and have a child who will be his heir. This man had six brothers and they all married her and died before they had children, whose wife will she be in heaven? First, they did not know the Scriptures. Jesus said, "The sons of this age marry and are given in marriage. He is saying that as long as we are in the flesh, we are free to marry or not. But if you are worthy to be in the first resurrection from the dead, then you will be in the Spirit, not in the flesh. You will not need to procreate for there will never be any death. People in heaven will not marry but will have a new glorified body. When we are raised from the dead, Jesus said we will be sons of God, and we will be equal with the angels. We will not be angels, just equal with them. Will you know your wife in heaven? Yes, you will, but you will not be married as you were in the flesh.

While we were on the subject of marriage, we asked Jesus if it was okay for us to get married. He said it was lawful and he wished us all happiness and hoped we would continue to serve Him.

(Mary) I had also asked Joanna if was it possible to be happy and to travel with Jesus. She had told me that it was possible and that Nathan and I would make a very good team working for the Lord. She also asked me more questions about our relationship than Jesus did. He seemed to know it was all right with us. She wanted to know what I saw in Nathan and if I loved him. I told her he was the most wonderful person in the world except Jesus. I had never known anyone who had so much knowledge about our Lord, and I know for a fact that he loves Jesus, and he also loves me. She said, "You didn't answer my question. I said do you love him?" My answer was a resounding "Yes, yes, yes!" However, we have decided to delay the marriage until after the Passover. Nathan will tell you why.

(Nathan) First of all the city of Jerusalem is crowded during the Passover. Then there is the uncertainty of what will happen to Jesus. We think he may be killed. We have tried to talk him out of attending but we cannot persuade him otherwise. I hope we can be married just as soon as things get back to normal. I must say that I have never seen anyone so dedicated to Jesus as Mary. She also makes me feel like there is no other woman in the world. I could never love anyone as I love her. We have one more story about Jesus. We hope you like it.

Luke 20:41-44

Jesus challenged the Pharisees by asking," How can David call his descendants Lord?" David under the inspiration of the Holy Spirit had called Jesus Lord. If David had called him Lord, then he must be God. The Pharisees had a way of not answering a question when it proved that Christ was Israel's Messiah. Then in the hearing of all the people, and there were a lot of them in the temple that day, 'Jesus said, "Beware of the Scribes who go around in long robes, loving greetings in the marketplace, and getting the best seats in the Synagogues, and the best places at the feasts. Who devour widow's houses, and for a pretense make long prayers." These will receive the greater condemnation." The Scribes and Pharisees claimed to be the official interrupters of the Mosaic Law. They demanded obedience in their teaching. Their message was to follow us we have the law. They loved long robes for attention, and they got it. They were all puffed up as saying, "Look at us we are holy." When they went into the synagogue, they chose the best seats so they could be seen. At the entire feast, they were there as if to say, that they made it official and that God approved of it. They did not practice the Law. They used it to impress the people. Christ condemned them and they hated Him. Lord, we are scared of what will happen in Jerusalem.

Chapter 33

ANDREW, BROTHER OF PETER

HEROD'S TEMPLE

Luke 21:1—19

We were all in the temple for most of the day. I just couldn't comprehend all Jesus was doing. It was as if he had to teach all day. He would go to the temple early in the morning and stay till almost dark. Then we would go to the Mount of Olives which was down from the temple mount and across the Kidron Brook and then up on the Mount of Olives. We camped there every night. He looked exhausted all the time. We tried to tell him to rest but he would not slow down.

We were sitting in Herod's' temple watching people. This Temple was the most magnificent building of our time. It seemed that someone was working on it all the time. It had shining white stone and lots of it was gold-covered. It shined so bright that one could see it was miles away. I could go on and on about how large and beautiful this temple was and how Herod the Great had so much interest in it.

Perhaps one could say the wickedest man of our time had built the most beautiful temple of our time. We were watching the rich put their gifts into the treasury. Then a widow woman came by and put in two mites which wasn't much money at all, so Jesus said, "Truly I say unto you that this poor widow has put in more than all, for all of these out of their abundance have put in offerings for God, but she out of her poverty put in all the livelihood she had." I took his meaning to be that it cost her more to give her two mites than it costs the rich. Therefore, her gift was more precious than theirs.

Then someone spoke about the temple just how beautiful it was adorned with stones and donations. Jesus also commented on this as well. He said, "These things that you see, the days will come and which not one stone shall be left upon another that shall not be thrown down." We were amazed at what he said and talked with each other privately as to what would happen to cause someone to destroy such a lovely building as this. When we were back on the Mount of Olives that evening, we could see the temple and never get tired of looking at it. Then we encouraged Peter to ask him what and when this would happen, and what sign would be given. Then we were told what was going to happen in the future. We were not prepared for all the things he told us but, we were still learning. First, he warned us not to be deceived for many people will come in his name saying he is the Christ. He said not to go after them. Secondly, he said there would be wars and rumors of wars. And he said not to fear for these things must come to pass but the end will not come immediately. Third, the nation will rise against nation, and kingdom against kingdom, with earthquakes, famines, pestilences, and fearful sights, and great signs from heaven.

"But before all these things happen, they will lay their hands on you and persecute you and drag you to jail and prison." You will go before kings and rulers because you are preaching in my name. But it will give you an opportunity to tell everyone about me. Promise me right now that you will not worry about what to say for, I will give you the words and wisdom that the adversaries will not be able to contradict. You will be betrayed by your parents, brothers, relatives, and friends and some of you will be put to death. Every one of you will be hated because you believe in me. But not a hair on your head will be lost. Stay with me to the end and you will be saved."

Wow was all I could say. Here I thought we 12 were not very important, but we were to carry the load he was carrying after he is gone. I felt fear; I felt like how will we twelve hold up after he is gone? He has told us that he would be killed and now he tells us of all these things that would come upon us, and he will not be here to shield us. Oh God, I feel so small and helpless that we need a helper.

The Destruction of Jerusalem
Luke 21: 20-24

He continued to tell us what the future would be like for our beloved city. He told us Jerusalem would one day be surrounded by armies, and then know that its destruction is near. It sounded like there will be lots of armies in that destruction. In fact, he said that all people who were living in Jerusalem should flee to the mountains. And let those who are in the city depart. And all who are in the country not to go near her. He also told us that these days were the days of vengeance so that all that is written in the scriptures may be fulfilled. These times were so bad that he pronounced a woe on all women who were pregnant and all who were nursing babies. For the distress in the land will be great, and great wrath will be upon the people. Those who do not escape from Jerusalem will be killed by the sword and some will be led away captive into all nations. Jerusalem will be trampled by the Gentiles until the times of the Gentiles are fulfilled. It sounded like the Jewish Kingdom would come to an end and Gentiles would be in charge for who knows how long. I think our God must be very angry with his chosen people.

The Coming of the Son of Man
Luke 21:25—58

What will be the signs? Signs in the sun, moon, and stars? There will be great distress on the earth and on all nations. Men have heart failures because of all the things happening. What are the terrible things that are happening? Earthquakes, the sun turning black as sackcloth of hair. The moon will look like blood. Stars will fall to the earth. The sky will recede like a scroll, and every mountain and island will move out of its place. All the kings and rich people will hide themselves in caves and in the rocks of the mountains. They will wish that the rocks and caves would fall on them. They wanted to be hidden from the face of Jesus, and from his wrath. For the great day of his Wrath has come and who is able to stand. All I can say about this is that I hope and pray that I will not be here when all these things happen. Then he gives us some other signs that we can count on, the fig tree (since we have so many of them here) and all the trees.

First, we see the buds and we know summer is coming. Then when we see all the signs, he has told us about, the kingdom of God is very near. Just as sure as we know leaves will appear and blooms will appear, and fruit will come later. In fact, it will happen in that generation. We have his word on it.

We are to keep watching and be careful that we don't forget. We have the whole world and all the pleasures of the world to keep us entertained. He mentions drunkenness carousing and the cares of this life. These habits can snare us and snatch our attention from God and help us to take on the burdens of the world. We are to watch and pray that we will be worthy to escape all these things and most of all we are to remember that all people will have to stand in judgment before the son of man.

It sounds like all these things are going to happen here in the land of Israel. All Israelites should be watching and praying that they will be worthy to escape all of these things that will come up to this nation. Jesus would go to the temple early every morning, he would teach there all day long, and then at night, he went out to the Mount of Olives. Then the next morning he would be back in the temple again and very many people came to hear him.

Chapter 34

JOHN, THE BROTHER OF JAMES
THE PLAN TO KILL JESUS

Luke 22:1—6

The Feast of the Passover and the Day of unleavened bread were the same. Some called it Passover and others refer to it as the days of unleavened bread. There were 7 days of the Passover we ate unleavened bread all that week. We would search the house for any yeast and if any was found it was removed. The house was clean to make sure. The Jews had added another day to the Passover and they called it the preparation day. The chief priest and the Scribe sought how they might kill Jesus. They wanted to do it discreetly so as not to stir up all the people who had come to Jerusalem for the Feast of the Passover. Then Satan entered Judas Iscariot and he went to the Chief Priest and Scribes to see how much they would pay him to betray Jesus. Poor Judas, a good businessman always knew how to make money sold out to the enemy. He agreed to look for an opportunity to betray Jesus somehow away from the multitude. I think he agreed to be a witness also.

Preparations for the Passover
Luke 22: 7-13

When the day of unleavened bread finally came, we were all excited about what was about to happen. Where would we eat the Passover meal? We had not bought a Passover Lamb. But Jesus already had it all planned out. He asked Peter and me to go into Jerusalem and prepare the Passover for us. He further told us that when we entered the city, we would meet a man carrying a picture of water, and follow him into the house. Then you are to ask the master of the house," The teacher wants to know where is the guest room where I may eat the Passover with my disciples?" Then he will show you a large furnished upper room. You are to make it ready.

We started looking for yeast and found none. The master of the House had already done all the work and we were just making sure that it was all done according to the instructions God gave Moses.

Here is a summary of what Peter and I did this morning we would go to the temple to purchase the lamb and then take it to the priest who inspected it. The lamb must be a one-year-old male. In the afternoon the lamb would be killed in the temple court and offered at the altar. The blood was poured on the altar and some of the Lamb was sacrificed and the rest taken home wrapped in its skin. It would be roasted for the feast. The menu would be unleavened cakes, bitter herbs, crushed fruit with vinegar, and roast lamb. We worked every minute and tried to be first as much as possible but it was impossible to be first because there were about 250,000 lambs slaughtered for this Passover and everyone was trying to be first in line. As Darkness was almost upon us, we had help, For the 12 had shown up with Jesus and we were permitted to go to the public bath for a much-needed refreshing bath. When we came back the food was ready to be served.

Jesus Institutes the Lord's Supper
Luke 22:14–23

We heard a blast from the silver trumpets in the temple announcing to all of Jerusalem that the Passover had arrived. We were in the upper room and we 12 were sitting down when Jesus spoke. "With fervent desire, I have desired to eat this Passover with you before I suffer. For I say to you I will no longer eat of it until it is fulfilled in the kingdom of God."

He also took the cup of wine and told us to divide it among ourselves. Then he informed us that he would not drink of the fruit of the vine until the kingdom of God comes. After supper, he did something different which has become known as the Lord's Supper. Some call it communion. Others call it the new covenant in his blood. Here is what he said and did that night in the upper room after we had observed the Passover. He took the bread, gave thanks, broke it, and gave it to us, saying, "This is my body which is given for you, do this in remembrance of me." Likewise, he took the cup after supper saying, "This cup is the new covenant in my blood which is shed for you." We were caught off guard, he often said and did things we did not understand. Some of the unleavened bread left from the Passover meal was used, and so was the wine. We had plenty of bread and wine. All of Israel had bread and wine daily. This bread was his body, broken for us. We did not know what it was about, but I do remember another time when he said something about eating flesh and drinking blood. I had to make mental notes of what he said. (John 6:53) "Then Jesus said to them most assuredly I say to you unless you eat the flesh of the son of, man and drink his blood you have no life in you." (John 6:54) "Whoever eats my flesh and drinks my blood has eternal life. And I will raise him up at the last day." So, there were lots of things going on at the feast and before I could ask Jesus about it, he said his betrayer was at this table. We did not know at the time that it was Judas. Peter was sitting far away from me because he was at the other end of the table. He remembered Jesus telling us that it was better to serve and that we were not to be like others and take the best seats. And we were not to wear clothing to get attention. Since he was looking my way and caught my eye, he motioned for me to find out who it was. So, I asked Jesus who it was and he said," he whom I give the sop to." Then he gave it to Judas. It was after he had been crucified and raised from the dead that I had time to think about all he said to us concerning his suffering and death on the cross.

Our group of followers of Jesus started to discuss his covenant which was written in his blood. Which he called his body and his blood. He had said to do this in remembrance of him. Some said in remembrance of his death. Others said it was to remember him and dying on the cross, and some said to remember he is God's son. Someone wanted to have bread and wine every time we met. Some homes set out bread and wine for the remembrance, while others had no money for bread and wine so we decided to do it only once a week. Others said the Passover was only once a year and that was the way we should do it. We really did not have any instruction on how often we should celebrate the Lord's Supper. Have you ever been in a group of people where everyone had a good idea but there was no way we could carry out all those ideas? I am talking about the days before we received the Holy Spirit. You might say we were a dysfunctional family; we did not communicate. We did not trust each other. Sometimes our emotions got the best of us. We had seen Jesus after he was resurrected and we were so overjoyed at seeing him that we did not ask him to teach us what to do now. We wrestled with the problem sometimes with resentment, but we stuck together trying to do what was right. Someone said," What would Jesus do?" Finally, after 50 days when the holy spirit came, we started to remember what he had told us, and we became new people. It must be what Jesus told Nicodemus that night, we must be born again. Born of the spirit, every follower of Jesus received the Holy Spirit. Now we remember the words of Jesus. How had we forgotten so much?

We started to work in unison and things were working better. Concerning the communion, we remembered what Jesus said, "This is my body which is given for you, do this in remembrance of me. This cup is the new covenant in my blood which is shed for you."

I think the bread and wine are bread and wine to us. But it is a symbol of flesh and blood. If he is happy with it that way then we will continue to do it for the rest of our lives. For he has said earlier that," whoever eats my flesh and drinks my blood has eternal life, and I will raise him up at the last day."

Now every time we have communion or Lord's Supper, we are to remember his death for the remission of sins. It is also for us to renew our commitment to him, and to recall his new covenant. Only Jesus has the authority to Institute a new covenant sealed in his blood.

Chapter 35

JOHN, THE BROTHER OF JAMES
MEN OR CHILDREN

Luke 22:63-65

As we look back at the Lord's Supper, we realize just how unruly we were. What must he have thought of us? It must have reminded him of children who were all the time bickering. I am so ashamed because it was such a sacred time and such an important time and we were squabbling like little children. Who is going to be the greatest? We were sure his kingdom would come soon. He had just said he would not drink the fruit of the vine until the kingdom of God came. He had reminded us that we were acting like Gentiles. We wanted to Lord it over others. We wanted a higher position. My own mother had asked him for high positions for my brother and me. He reminded us that to be honored we must become servants. Christ was the son of God; he was acting as the servant of the Lord. He did not seek honor. In fact, he later washed our feet just as a servant would do. He told us that we had continued with him in his trials, and because of our faithfulness he would appoint us positions of honor and his kingdom. Our positions would be determined by our faithful service. He had already told us that his father had granted him a kingdom and he had granted us a place there also. He said we would eat and drink at his table and sit on thrones and judge the 12 tribes of Israel.

Just then he told Simon Peter that Satan has asked for him but I have prayed that his faith will not fail. Why Peter? Most likely because Peter was a born leader a little impulsive but he could be counted on. Just like Peter the impulsive he said," Lord I am ready to go with you both to prison and to death." Then Jesus said to him," I tell you Peter the cock will not crow this day before you will deny three times that you know me." The blood seemed to rush to Peter's head for he turned very red. I wondered what was going to happen if Peter would deny that he even knew Christ. Well, you know the rest of the story; Peter did deny that he knew Christ three times. Jesus told us that when he sent us out to proclaim his name to the house of Israel the kingdom was near. We did not take money, sleeping bags, or sandals, and we lacked nothing. Now when we were to go out, we must take all these things, plus a sword and garments. Simon Peter pulled out of his sword and Simon the Zealot also had one, and Jesus said that it was enough. We all went out from the upper room and climbed the Mount of Olives. Jesus was ready to pray. We were instructed to pray for ourselves that we would not enter into temptation. He went about a stone's throw away and knelt down to pray for Himself. I heard Him say, "Father if it is your will take this cup from me." Then an angel appeared and gave Him strength. Then He prayed some more and came and found us asleep. We all had had a long and tiring day and we could not stay awake.

Jesus Betrayed by Judas
Luke 22:47-53

He told us to rise and pray again so that we wouldn't fall into temptation. Almost immediately a large group of people burst upon the scene. Judas Iscariot was with them. He had betrayed Jesus with a kiss. Peter pulled his small sword and cut off the ear of the servant on the high priest. Jesus told us to put away our swords. He also healed the wounded man. He asked that we be not harmed and they led him away to beat and shame him. Simon Peter followed at a distance. A fire was burning in the courtyard and Peter came to warm himself when a servant girl saw him and said, "You are also one of them." But Peter said, "Woman I am not." About an hour later someone else said this man was one of them. And Peter said I am not. Then another said this man was with him for he is a Galilean, Peter said" Man I do not know what you are saying." Then immediately the rooster crowed. Christ looked up and Peter saw him and he remembered the words Christ had spoken to him and he went out and wept bitterly.

The men who held Jesus mocked and beat him. They blindfolded him and struck him in the face while asking him to prophesy who struck him. This is just one of the many things they did to him.

The Sanhedrin
Luke 22:66-71

When the day started to break a chief priest and scribes came and led him to the Sanhedrin. They asked him if he was the Christ. He said, "If I told you, you would not believe me. They asked him if he was the son of God. He answered, "You rightly say that I am." They said they needed no further testimony, for we have heard it from His own mouth. The illegal trials had already convicted him before he came to this council. This trial was only a show. No trials are to happen at night. So says the Jewish Law.

They called no witnesses at this trial. They made no effort to find any. Their minds were made up before giving Judas the 30 pieces of silver.

They said "This trial is over; we don't need any testimony. We have heard it from His own mouth." They could hardly wait to get him to Pilate. I went along with the crowd and no man questioned me.

Jesus Handed to Pilate
Luke 23:1-7

The mob of priests, elders, and scribes took Jesus from the council to Pilate the governor of Judea he lived in Caesarea on the Seacoast. He came to Jerusalem for the Jewish Passover. Pilate was known as a cruel ruthless man. He did not like anyone, especially Jews. They were sure that he would be glad they put Jesus to death. He was not up and he was angry when he came to talk. His talk was insulting and, in a hurry, to get rid of us. The priests, elders, and scribes, change their stories about Jesus. They knew that Pilate was not interested in Jesus insulting the religious leaders. They said," We found this man perverting the nation. They said Jesus had insisted the nation not pay taxes to Caesar. They said Jesus claimed to be the king in opposition to Caesar. Pilate asks Jesus if he was King of the Jews. Jesus was standing before Pilate completely worn out. He was also a bloody mess. He did not in any way look like a king to Pilate. Pilate was not alarmed by the appearance of Jesus. He certainly was not a threat to Rome. His question could have been, (You King of the Jews?) Jesus finally spoke and answered," It is as you say."

To everyone, Pilate said," I find no fault in this man." To this crowd, it was as if we couldn't believe our own ears. They started raising their voice and became fiercer, and he stirred up the people from Judea to Galilee."

Jesus Before Herod
Luke 23:6-12

Now Pilate breathed a sigh of relief for he knew King Herod was in this city of Jerusalem, not because he was a Jew but because he brought troops to help control the people. He quickly sent him to King Herod so as to get him off his hands. Pilate had said I find no fault with him.

When Herod saw Jesus, he was very happy because he had heard so much about him. What he had heard was Jesus was doing miracles or magic tricks and he wanted to see one. Not only that but he had heard Jesus was telling everyone that he was a king. Herod looked him over and saw that he was not a threat. He sure did not look like a king. Jesus looked like he was exhausted, sleepy, and not impressed with King Herod. He asked Jesus question after question but Jesus did not answer him. The chief priests and teachers of the law were there accusing him of all kinds of crime. Then Herod and his soldiers began to ridicule and mock him hoping he would say something in his own defense, but he would not open his mouth. Then they dressed him up in an elegant robe to look like a king and sent him back to Pilate.

Herod Sends Jesus Back to Pilate
Luke 23:13-25

Herod did not find Jesus guilty, for he would not have sent him back to Pilate. Pilate and Herod had been enemies now they have become friends. When we got back to Pilate's house Pilate was still agitated and told the priests and religious leaders, he found no fault in him. He had done nothing worthy of death. So as to please the crowd he offered to chastise him and release him after all I find no fault in this man and neither did Herod. I thought if Jesus is innocent of any crime why punish him? But they not only were going to punish him lightly but to scourge him with a whip. This type of punishment was for hardened criminals and Jesus was an innocent man. 39 lashes with a whip were severe. Sometimes it killed the person. His back look like raw flesh after it was done. It was customary that one criminal was to be released at the feast so Pilate was willing to release Jesus when the subject of releasing a prisoner was brought up. They had a man named Barabbas who was a murderer and a rebellious person. Then Pilate gave them a choice and they wanted to release Barabbas and to crucify Jesus. They yelled crucify him. Then for the third time, Pilate pleaded with the crowd why, what has he done? I find no reason for death for him. Pilate was really trying to defend Jesus. The crowd was insistent and demanded with a loud voice crucify him. Those loud voices convince Pilate to have Jesus crucified just as they had requested.

They also freed Barabbas. When justice is perverted by the instance of a crowd of people then that is not justice but mob rule. This kind of justice will eventually bring down a nation. As for the sentence, God knows that Jesus was born to die for the sins of the world even the evil people who had Jesus crucified.

Chapter 36

JOHN, THE BROTHER OF JAMES
THE CROSS AND THE KING

Luke 23:26_32

As Jesus was led away to the cross of crucifixion his condition was not good at all. He had been beaten and his face was bloody from the crown of thorns. He had been stripped of his clothes. He had been in the hands of his enemy for twelve hours, from nine until nine. From Thursday until Friday.

The emotional stress was also upon him like no other has ever experienced. The loss of blood, the abandonment of the disciples, and the sleepless night were too much for him. He had been forced to walk about two and one-half miles, and the knowledge that he was to have nails pierce his hands and feet was surely taking a toll on him. All he had was his life, and he gladly went marching toward his death.

He had to carry the cross beam through the streets of Jerusalem and up the hill to the place of crucifixion. He went quietly like a lamb, for he was the Lamb of God who came to take away the sins of the world.

The cross beam he was carrying weighed seventy-five to one hundred pounds. It was placed just outside the city wall, for people to see when they passed by. When he was made to pick it up, he could not handle it. Then he fell and the Roman soldiers put it on the back of one Simon who was from Cyrene, a town in north Africa. He was young and strong and able to walk just behind Jesus to the crucifixion. Oh, how I would have gladly carried his cross if I had the chance.

A Roman guard led the procession with a sign that said," This is the King of the Jews." A great multitude of people followed Jesus, People who loved him and people who hated him. All along the way there were curious people. Some of the women mourned for him, but Jesus turned to them and said, "Daughters of Jerusalem, do not weep for me, but for yourselves and your children, for indeed the days are coming in which they will say, "Blessed are the barren wombs that never bore, and breasts that never nursed," Luke 23: 28-29.

That same day they crucified two criminals with Jesus one on his left side and one on his right at a place called Calvary

They threw him to the ground which was easy because he was out of energy, and he never resisted anything they wanted to do to him. So, he was laid on his back on the wooden beam which they had nailed to the crossbar, his arms were stretched out and tied to the crossbars so he could not move while they drove the nails through his hands. There was more blood coming from his hands plus his back started bleeding also. Oh, how my heart cried out for him wondering how he was still living.

Then they drove long nails through his feet and even more blood was spilled on the ground below the cross. His cross was about three feet above the ground, and the cross of the criminal was about two feet. The sign above Jesus said he was King of the Jews.

As they were casting lots for His clothing, he was praying for the poor fellow below him saying, "Father, forgive them for they do not know what they do."

I needed to bring Jesus' mother closer for she and the other ladies, Mary, wife of Cleophas, and Mary Magdalene were happy to see me. I asked them if they were strong enough to move closer and see his suffering and they said "Yes." I am told the two criminals had a conversation with him while I was talking to the women from Galilee. One of those had ridiculed Him and the other asked Jesus to remember him when he came into his kingdom and Jesus had told him that today he would be with him in paradise.

When Jesus saw us, he spoke and said, "Woman behold your son." And he said to me, "Behold your mother." From that time on she lived in my house and we were happy to have her.

Then he said," I thirst". He was given sour wine on a sponge. Then he said," It is finished." and he gave up his Spirit.

The centurion saw what happened and said, "Certainly this was a righteous man." (Luke 23:47), and the whole crowd that had come to see the sight went home. We four were joined by other people from Galilee who loved Jesus and followed him.

Someone said we must leave and make preparations for his burial. However, we did not know that Joseph of the council had made arrangements. He had gone and asked for the body of Jesus. He took it down, wrapped it in linen, and laid it in a tomb that was hewn out of rock, where no one had ever been laid before. We had to hurry for the Sabbath was just a couple of hours away. Some of the women from Galilee were helping along with Nicodemus. They hurried so they would have time to prepare the spices for his body as soon as the Sabbath was over.

I Wish I Could Have Helped Jesus

I wish I could have helped Jesus
When he was born that night
With a nice warm blanket
It's only what's right

I wish I could have helped Jesus
It's the least I could do
Just tell those Roman soldiers
He loves everybody, even you

I wish I could have helped Jesus
Wipe his blood from his thorny crown
If possible, there was a way
I could just get him out of town

I wish I could have helped Jesus
When they gave him vinegar and gall
I could have given him cool water
Shown him I care, that's all

I wish I could have helped Jesus
When he was crucified that day
When he cried out "Father forgive"
He took all our sins away

There was no way I could have helped Jesus
But he sure has helped me
I now have a Manson in glory
Where I will spend eternity

Chapter 37

PETER, BROTHER OF ANDREW
THE MYSTERY OF THE MISSING BODY

Luke 24: 1-53

Very early on the first day of the week_ even before it was daylight the ladies from Galilee came to the tomb bringing spices to rewrap his body. They found the stone rolled away and they entered and found no one. They seemed to panic, so they ran back to where John and I were staying, saying his body was missing.

Luke 24:10

The ladies who told the two of us were Mary Magdalene, Joanna, Mary Mother of James, and other women who were from Galilee. We did not believe the women. Lots of people do not believe in the resurrection of Jesus but I was at a loss as to what to say. I kept thinking the guards who were watching the tomb would know. They thought he would rise from the dead so they sealed the tomb and put a guard there. The women said they went into the tomb and found two men in shining robes so bright that it hurt their eyes. The women were terrified and bowed low before them. The men in the bright robes ask them why are looking in a tomb for someone who is alive, they said he isn't here he came back to life again. Don't you remember he told you this while you were back in Galilee? He said he must be betrayed into the hands of an evil man and be crucified and that he would rise again on the third day. Then the woman remembered and rushed back to tell everyone what had happened and what the two men said about him.

They met John and me on the way to the tomb. We thought they were telling stories like fairy tales. Now the two of us ran the rest of the way to the tomb. John was younger and more energetic than I was, so He ran ahead of me and stopped at the door of the empty tomb. However, he looked inside and saw the empty tomb with linen wrappings laying just as if they were on someone. Then I came huffing and puffing up behind him and saw the clothes lying there and also the napkin that had covered Jesus' face all rolled up in a bundle and lay at the side. Then John said he believed that Jesus was raised from the dead. I sort of thought the same thing, something like wishful thinking. We did not know the Holy Scriptures that said he would rise from the dead. There are records of 11 appearances before his ascension and three after. Most likely there were others that are not recorded.

He first appeared to Mary of Magdala. She was seeking his body and she found it. He was alive and well. She was at the graveside and he spoke her name and she knew him immediately. He said for her not to touch him for he had not yet ascended to his father. But to go and tell my brother that I ascend to my father and your father and to my God and to your God. Then Mary passed these words along to the disciples. Then that very same evening being the first day of the week when the doors were shut and locked and the disciples were assembled for fear of the Jews, Jesus came and stood in our midst. We were afraid and surprised, we were glad. We saw him stand here before us and said," Peace be unto you." He wasted no time but showed us his hands and his side and we were both happy and sad. He brought back the memories of his suffering and for this we were sad. But the nails scarred hands and this spear-torn side also were proof for sure that he was a person and not a ghost,

He also said as the father has sent me, even so, I send you. Then he breathed on us and said receive you the Holy Spirit. Then my mind and understanding opened up. I started to recall what he had said to us in Galilee. After 8 days he showed up again. We were a different group now. All believed he was the Messiah; all believe he was God's son; all believed that he was raised from the dead. Oops. We all believed except one. His name is Thomas. He had not been with us when Jesus appeared to the 10 apostles and lots of other believers. He had not received the Holy Spirit He said," I just cannot believe until I see his hands and put my fingers into the nail prints and thrust my hand into his side. It happened on this particular day Thomas was with us when Jesus came just as he did the last time. He said, "Peace to you again," and then he turned to Thomas and said, "Reach your fingers and put them in my hands, and put your hand into my side and don't be faithless any longer, believe." Thomas was overwhelmed and could only say, my Lord and my God. Then Jesus said," You believe because you have seen me, blessed are those who haven't seen me and believe anyway." Now you all have read about Jesus telling us to meet him in Galilee and as yet we have not made it back home. Before this meeting was over, we disciples and apostles decided it was time to go home and see our families and meet Jesus some place in Galilee. John will tell you the rest of that story.

Chapter 38

JOHN, BROTHER OF JAMES

FISH FOR BREAKFAST

John 21:1—25

We all decided it was time to go back to Galilee. We had quite a group of both men and women. Even some children were with us, and we all had a fun trip home. When we would leave our homes in Galilee to go up to Jerusalem to keep the Passover or go for any other feast such as the Feast of the Tabernacles, we would go rejoicing for we were going to meet the Lord. On the way home we decided we were going to meet the Lord and we should be rejoicing. And so, we did. That made the trip pleasant. We could rejoice because we were going back home. Oh, there's no feeling like going home. Our families would be expecting us. We had a wonderful reunion and caught up on the news. We had to answer so many questions that we were talking all the time.

Finally, a few days later it seemed all the questions were answered, and we men were gathered on the seashore and talked about meeting with Jesus. No one knew when, where, or how it was going to happen. It was getting dark, and Peter said he was going fishing. Now our group had some experience fishermen. There was Simon Peter, Thomas the twin, Nathaniel from Cana in Galilee, my brother James and two other disciples. I think there were seven of us. We all said," We will come too." We fished all night, and we caught nothing. At about dawn, we were almost to the beach when we saw a man standing on the beach. He called out," Have you any fish men? No, we said." Then throw your nets on the right side of the boat and you will catch plenty of them. Peter tossed the nets just like he said. We caught so many fish we were struggling to pull the nets in.

I thought how does he know where the fish are? Then I thought it must be Jesus.

I told Peter it must be the Lord. As quick as a wink he put on his tunic. Then he jumped into the water. The rest of us stayed in the boat and wrestled with getting the fish in the boat, but we couldn't. So, we dragged them towards the shore and Peter, who was on land now, came in to help pull the net the rest of the way. We then saw that there was a fire and fish was cooking and he also had bread.

This was the third appearance of Jesus since his appearance from the dead. Jesus asked us to bring some of the fish we had caught. Simon Peter counted the fish and there were 153 large fish now we would have rejoiced at a large number of fish we had caught, but Jesus was there and we wanted to see him, He said something like come on children breakfast is ready, so we gathered around Jesus at the fire on the Sea shore of Galilee and had a breakfast we will never forget. He had provided for us for about 3 years, and now he was showing us that he could still provide for us. Hallelujah, what a savior.

After breakfast, Jesus said to Simon Peter," Simon's son of John do you love me more than these others? "Yes, Peter said you know that I love you." Feed my Lambs" Jesus told him. Then Jesus said," Simon son of John do you really love me?", Peter said," Yes Lord you know that I love you." Jesus said, "Take care of my sheep." Once more Jesus said to Simon Peter," Simon son of John do you really love me?" Peter was grieved that Jesus asked the same question the third time. He said," Lord you know my heart you know all things and Jesus said," Then feed my sheep."

"When you were young you were able to do as you lacked and go where you wanted, but when you are old you will stretch out your hands and others will direct you and take you where you do not want to go". Jesus said this to let him know what kind of death he would die to glorify God. Then Jesus said," Follow me." Peter turned around and saw me and said to Jesus," What about him Lord what sort of death will he die?" Jesus, said" If I want him to live until I return what is that to you?" I haven't written all Jesus said and I suppose if everything he said was written the whole world could not hold all the books. There were many more things recorded by Matthew and Mark. He would show up when we were not expecting him. After our time with Jesus in and around Galilee, we were instructed to go back to Jerusalem.

. We had some good times with Jesus and our families and lots of friends. Naturally, we told a lot of people that Jesus was the Messiah of Israel, and numerous Pharisees also believed in him. Not only because we said so but because of the records that Joseph and Nicodemus had sent to the Sanhedrin. Then they had plenty of time to patiently tell their story and experience while traveling with us.

This also gave us a base of believers in Jerusalem as well as all the little towns south of the Sea of Galilee. When we were on our way to Jerusalem, we stopped and caught them up on all the appearances of Jesus after his resurrection.

Fishing

Come on men and let's go fishing
Come on men and let's go fishing
Come on men and let's go fishing
We'll have a good ole time
We'll have a good ole time

We'll catch those fish and put 'em in the boat
We'll catch those fish and put em' in the boat
We'll catch those fish and put em' in the boat
We'll have a good, ole time
We'll have a good, ole time

We fished all night and we caught nothing
We fished all night and we caught nothing
We fished all night and we caught nothing
And we didn't have a good ole time
And we didn't have a good ole time

Cast your nets on the right side of the boat
Cast your nets on the right side of the boat
Cast your nets on the right side of the boat
And you'll have a good, ole time
And you'll have a good, ole time

Come on children, breakfast is ready
Come on children, breakfast is ready
Come on children, breakfast is ready
We'll have a good ole time
We'll have a good ole time

When you go fishing, take along Jesus
When you go fishing, take along Jesus
When you go fishing, take along Jesus
You'll have a good ole time
You'll have a good ole time

William H Stephens

Epilogue

LUKE

Acts 1
Birth of the Church

My dear friend and lover of God: I hope my letters have kept you informed about all the information I collected about Jesus, Son of God and Son of Man. This is an account as told to me by people who knew him personally and worked with him for almost 3 years. This was the most exciting thing I have ever done. It's like I was with Jesus and his 12-plus others who truly loved him and could spend time with him. I have learned to love Israel and her people. But most of all I have loved Jesus Christ. I am now in Antioch with Paul and Barnabas and many believers. Some of them are from Israel and have found jobs. I thought you should know about what happened during the last days Jesus was on earth. He was here 40 days after his crucifixion and appeared to his disciples many times to prove to them that he was indeed the Son of GOD. He also taught the Old Testament, for the prophets and the Psalms spoke of him and how all those prophecies had come to pass. He told everyone to stay in Jerusalem until the

Holy Spirit came and baptized them. He said that when the Holy Spirit has come upon you, you will have the power to testify about me. They were to start in Jerusalem and Judea and even Samaria and to the ends of the earth, telling this wonderful story about the life, death, burial, and resurrection of the Son of God. They were to tell how believing in his name would wash away all our sins., That meant Jews, Greeks, Samaritans, and all people on earth no matter their color or what language they spoke.

He was walking with them on the Mount of Olives when he was taken up into the sky and disappeared. His friends were told that he would return someday just as he had left. Then they all walked back to Jerusalem and had a prayer meeting in an upper room the same room as they celebrated the last Passover.

This is a list of the disciples who were there: Peter, James and John, Andrew, Phillip, Thomas, Bartholomew, Matthew, James's son of Alpheus, Simon called the zealot. And Judas son of James, and the brothers of Jesus plus several women including his mother.

This prayer meeting went on for several days and was attended by about 120 people. The day of Pentecost arrived, and the believers were together when the church was born. Suddenly there was a great noise like a windstorm in the sky above them, then it looked like flames of fire or tongues of fire and settled on each believer, and everyone was filled with the Holy Spirit. They begin speaking in languages they did not know. This was a gift from the Holy Spirit. Lots of people there were of another nationality and spoke different languages, but they heard and understood because they were speaking their language. There were about 15 to 17 different languages spoken and all were perplexed at what was happening. Peter had to step forward and explain that God had visited them and had given them the Holy Spirit. He preached his best sermon by telling the story of Jesus, and he also spoke of King David.

The people were deeply moved and asked, "Brothers what must we do?" Peter said, "Turn from your sins," which meant repent. Return to God and be baptized in the name of our Lord Jesus Christ for the forgiveness of sins and you will receive the Holy Spirit. About

146

3,000 believed and were baptized and joined the other believers in regular attendance at the apostle's teaching, communion services, and prayer meetings. The apostles did many miracles as the believers met regularly and shared with one another.

There are some of those believers here in Antioch who are sharing the story of Jesus with all they meet. This will be my last letter for a while because I will be traveling with Paul and Barnabas on a journey. Blessing to you and your household and all who read this account of Jesus.

Your friend forever,
Luke

Printed in the United States
by Baker & Taylor Publisher Services